THE FLOOD

What People Are Saying About *The Flood*

"I was privileged to see *The Flood* soon after publication, and I am happy to report that I found it to be a gripping children's story that has a ring of authenticity that makes one suspect it is based on personal experience. The simple line illustrations are charmingly effective and add immeasurably to the reading experience."

–John Cooke, grandfather,
photographer, and nature writer

"The story is one of hope, determination, and empathy. Thoughtful strangers reach out to help others. The community effort to rebuild teaches that positive outcomes can arise from adversity. It also includes pets for us animal lovers. I am donating a copy of *The Flood* to our school library. I liked the illustrations and love the cover! You scared me when Goldie disappeared. So glad she didn't die. I would have been mad! Thank you, Wendy Bartlett, for new literature to share with our students!

–Beverly Tisdel,
assistant grade school teacher
and grandmother

"I liked the dialogue. The story runs smoothly and has a really good plot."

–Leo, age 10 3/4

"I thought it was well written and perfectly paced."

–Charlie, age 10 1/2

"Great bedtime story...crisp and short chapters that are full of adventure and have cliff hanger endings. Sweet fun."

–Gregory Baurmann, singer/songwriter

"Wonderful! The courage and resourcefulness of these three young girls are just what we want our grandchildren to read about and reflect upon. It's a gripping story leavened with humor. Imaginative, well-structured and beautifully crafted, it will engage the young reader in high adventure."

—Dean Curtis, writer, composer,
music teacher and grandmother

"I loved reading the Flood. Beautiful writing and each chapter ending sent me right on to the beginning of the next—like Charles Dickens! The three girls were beloved and strong beyond their years."

—Marilynn Rowland,
piano teacher, writer, mother of two

The Elizabeth Books

A Day at PreSchool
A Fun Place to Play with New Friends
A picture book to read to kids entering preschool

Elizabeth at School
A Safe Place to Learn
A picture book for ages 6 – 8

Elizabeth in Paris
Traveling with My Mom, the Artist
A picture book for ages 6 – 8

The Flood
The Dangerous Exploits of Three Girls, a Cat and a Boat
A chapter book for ages 9 – 12

The Elizabeth Books

THE FLOOD

The Dangerous Exploits of Three Girls, a Cat and a Boat

Written and Illustrated by
Wendy Bartlett

Kensington Hill Books
Berkeley, California

Kensington Hill Books
Berkeley, California

kensingtonhillbooks.com

Ordering Information:
Quantity sales. Special discounts are available on quantity purchases by schools, associations, and others. For details, contact the publisher via the Contact page on the above website.

The Flood: The Dangerous Exploits of Three Girls, a Cat and a Boat / Wendy Bartlett —1st ed.
ISBN 978-1-9449070-0-6 print
ISBN 978-1-9449070-1-3 ebook

Contents

Babysitting

Dad stood up and put the newspaper down on his chair. Mom and he walked over to where I was reading in my favorite, cozy reading chair. When she put her hand on my shoulder, she startled me, my brain being somewhere in the middle of the ocean. Laying down my book, *Island of the Blue Dolphins,* I looked around at Dad, then Mom.

"What, Mom?" I asked, partly closing my novel, and squinting up at her face.

"We're going to the town meeting at the Community Center," she said. "We won't be long. You can babysit Amanda for an hour, okay? Here's the video of *The Wizard of Oz* you two can watch again."

"Mom," I said, looking at the old video, "I'd rather read. Amanda can watch it, I suppose. But can't we come, too?" After all, I was eleven now! I pulled up my sock, and glanced over at Dad.

"We won't be long. You two would be very bored at that meeting, so just stay here with Mandy for a little while and we'll be back soon," Mom answered, smiling down at my deliberately scrunched-up, pretending-to-whine face.

"Yeah, I would be bored alright," added my four-year-old sister, Amanda, as she sat on the floor quietly reading to her teddy bear from her book, *Little Bear*.

I sprang up to go into the kitchen to get a snack.

"Well, okay, Mom, but bring us something special from town, even *The Lion King*. We're getting tired of *The Wizard of Oz*," I moaned, trying to make my eyes look bored to my mom. Amanda got up from the floor, walked over to us, and held my hand.

"Okay, Elizabeth, I'll check and see what's available," answered Mom, stroking my hair, her eyes looking straight into my pouting face. She reached over to Amanda and stroked her hair, too, and smiled at her the way she does at both of us.

"Now, you two have a good time together and we'll be back soon," she said, checking her cell phone as she kissed our upturned mouths.

"Okay, Mom, we'll be good," I said, walking with Mom and Dad across the living room. I punched Dad's shoulder as they walked past the staircase towards the front door. He swatted my backside. I twirled away from him.

"You'd better be good, you little rascals!" he said, wagging his finger with a smile, and disappearing with Mom through the front door.

"Okay, Mom. Okay, Dad, we'll be good," we echoed like we were singing a duet.

The sound of our car grew dimmer and dimmer as they drove through the countryside and faded away into the rainy night like the end of a song drifting towards a distant silence.

Darkness Everywhere

Right in the middle of *The Wizard of Oz*, the lights flickered out, the video stopped, and darkness enveloped us.

"Hey! What happened?" Amanda asked me.

"Oh, the electricity went out again," I sighed, sitting up straight and putting my book down. "It'll come back on in a minute. Remember last week, Amanda? It only took about three minutes to come back on."

We waited for a long, gloomy five minutes.

"Why isn't it back on now?" asked Amanda.

"It will be pretty soon," I comforted her, sinking into the couch, quietly sighing to myself.

We waited another five minutes. No lights, no video. Amanda's hand slid into mine and she snuggled a little closer to me.

After another twenty minutes, Amanda quietly lay down with her teddy bear. She sleepily said, "Wake me up when we can finish the movie." In a short while, her quiet breathing told me she was asleep.

Mom and Dad were not back, and I really didn't know what to do, so I decided to try the telephone number of the Community Center. I knew it by heart, because I had called Mom there a few times before. I counted the numbers on the phone across the top in their rows like a blind person, hoping I would push the right numbers. I knew from before that, even if the electricity was out, the land line would connect to their cell phone. But when I tried it this time, the phone wasn't working either. Holding my breath, I listened for the dial tone. It wasn't there, so I hung up. I couldn't help picking up the receiver once again and listening hopefully. Silence. I had never felt so alone.

I waited with my hand in its usual place supporting my chin, then switched to the other hand for a while, and then switched back again. I was determined not to cry, no matter what.

Amanda started to wiggle and turn and promptly rolled off the couch onto the floor.

"Hey, what happened? Elizabeth, are you there?" she asked, crawling back onto the couch and putting her hands all over my face.

"Sure, Amanda—haven't moved an inch. I tried to call the Community Center, but … the line's busy," I lied.

"Where's Mommy and Daddy?" she asked.

"They'll be back soon," I said, wondering if I were lying again.

"Well, I'm hungry," said Amanda, loudly.

"Okay, let's see if we can get to the kitchen," I answered.

Amanda felt around for her bear and we stood up and both scuffed our shoes over to the cold, dark wall and put our hands on it, inching our way along the hallway. We felt our way around the little wooden hall table and moved towards the kitchen.

We ventured slowly in the direction of the refrigerator. When I opened the fridge door, I couldn't see anything. I opened the freezer, felt the cold ice cube tray and grabbed the ice cream on top of it. I felt a spoon on the breadboard, grabbed it, and lunged into the ice cream container. I didn't know what flavor it was until I put the spoon on my tongue and let its coldness slide over my tongue like a sailboat on a wave.

"I'm having chocolate ice cream. Yum. Want some?" I asked Amanda, turning my head to that smaller, shadowy figure standing next to me.

"Nope. I want some milk and so does Bear."

Amanda nudged me to move over and opened the refrigerator door again and let her fingers move into the dark space where she felt for the milk. She pulled the half-gallon container off the shelf and grabbed for a cup from the dish drainer, knocking a plate over with a bang. I could hear her starting to pour the milk.

"Oh, no you don't. Let me do it for you, Amanda. It is too dark and I can do it without breaking stuff!" I told her, as I put my spoon down and reached over for the bottle.

"I didn't break anything," whined Amanda.

"Well, you almost did, so let me just do it, okay?" I gently shoved Amanda's side. Then I poured a cup full without spilling more than a drop, and handed it carefully to Amanda. She took a couple of gulps.

"Hey, Bear, you have a sip, too," she said.

We felt around the drainer for bowls. We found the granola and concocted a yummy bowl of granola with raisins, nuts and milk, and we ate every single bit of it. Then we put our bowls up to our mouths and got the very last drop of milk.

Because it was dark, I decided, without even talking about it, to go upstairs to our bedroom. But first, I got out a tray and felt all around the food shelves and found the peanut butter jar and the boxes of graham crackers, rye crackers and cheese crackers, and the half-gallon carton of milk and two glasses. Of course, the minute I picked up the tray, everything started to slide to one side.

"Here, Amanda, you carry the crackers, okay?"

"Okay," said Amanda. She sometimes liked to be my helper.

I felt around the kitchen counter and found the fruit bowl. Like an animal, I picked up the apple and sniffed it. The sweet smell made it into a real live apple dangling from a tree, swaying in the breeze and beckoning me to eat it. I sniffed the bananas and felt like a gorilla, then I handed them to Amanda, and she held them with one hand against her stomach next to the crackers and Bear. I put the sweet-smelling apples on the tray.

In the darkness we moved along like we were in slow motion, from the kitchen wall to the staircase, feeling our way against the cold wall with our shoulders and arms, and very slowly, starting to climb the stairs.

"Let's play a game!" I said. "Let's put one foot up and another foot up and then let's just stand still, okay!" I was afraid I was going to drop everything any minute. So, slowly, I put my left foot up one stair, then pulled the right foot up and placed it carefully next to my left foot. Looking up the stairs at the brighter area at the top of the staircase, I could hardly see where I was going. I steadied myself and balanced the tray like a circus acrobat. Amanda followed closely behind. Then, again, I put the left foot up one stair, and then my right foot up, and then we both rested, one stair apart. Amanda's warm breath puffed up onto the back of my arm.

"The bananas are slipping," whispered Amanda.

"Press harder on them, we're almost there," I whispered back to Amanda, the darkness demanding of us a quiet acknowledgement.

All the way up the stairs we kept up this slow rhythm, like a mommy and baby elephant, until we reached the top. Amanda touched my back with her elbow every other stair, a reassuring nudge.

"Wasn't that fun?" I said lightly.

"Yeah, that was really fun," answered Amanda, leaning her head against my arm.

"Oh, no," said Amanda loudly, forgetting to whisper.

"I dropped the bananas."

"Pick them up and don't bump me, we're almost there," I said, trying not to show any irritation.

Amanda held Bear and felt around on the floor. I could imagine her little body kneeling down to find the bananas and the crackers, then tucking Bear under her arm. I heard her say, "Got them!" as she picked up the bananas and crackers.

"Where did you go?" whined Amanda.

"I am standing right here."

"I can't see anything," she said, bumping right into me.

"Oh, there you are," said Amanda, giggling.

We took a few more tiny steps as carefully as we could and got into our bedroom and I was sure glad to put the tray down on my bed.

"Let's have a teddy bear party of crackers with peanut butter and milk," I suggested, listening to the rain beat against the window. I made sure my knee touched hers.

"Okay, here's Bear. Now you eat your cracker," she said to her bear, taking a bite herself.

After we ate, Amanda lay down.

"Elizabeth, are you there?"

"Yes, I am right here," I answered, touching her hair.

"Is Mommy coming home soon?" she asked.

"Of course she is," I said, trying to sound confident.

"Goodnight, Elizabeth," said Amanda in a soft, sleepy voice.

Amanda snuggled up to my leg on the bed and fell asleep again. I sat up waiting. I checked to see if Amanda was really asleep, and when I was sure she was, I couldn't help crying quietly to myself and wondering where our parents were.

Sometime in the middle of the long night, I guess I just slipped into a deep slumber, because I don't remember much else.

The Flood

The pounding of rain against the window outside awakened me in the morning. It sounded like people were throwing endless streams of pebbles against the window. I rushed into Mom and Dad's bedroom. Nobody was there. The bed was still made. I went back into our bedroom and looked out the window. At first all I could see was a wall of rain.

"Amanda, look," I said and put my head against the cold window.

"What?" answered Amanda, rubbing her eyes to wake up.

And then I knew what the night had brought us.

"I don't believe this!" I yelled as I saw that our house was now in the middle of nothing but water. "We're surrounded by water!" I exclaimed.

"Elizabeth, did Mommy come home?" asked Amanda, staggering over to the window, blinking against the cold glass.

"No, Amanda. I don't think they came back!" I said, wishing I didn't have to say that.

"What are we going to do now, Elizabeth?" moaned Amanda, taking my hand.

"I don't really know just yet," I answered, shrugging my shoulders while Amanda shrugged her little shoulders, too.

She went to pick up her teddy bear and whispered in her ear, "Don't worry, we'll think of something." She looked up at me. I sank onto the floor, crossed my legs, and planted my hand firmly under my chin while my other hand scratched my head.

I got up after a hard think, and we both sat down on the bed again and waited and waited.

Amanda kept watching me. I wiped away a tear from my face while I hugged Amanda. Amanda sniffed and held my hand. Every so often we ate more crackers and peanut butter, and drank some milk.

"Would you read to me, Elizabeth?" asked Amanda, holding out several books.

"Okay, but you'd better listen to me this time," I answered, remembering how easily Amanda went to sleep whenever I read her a story.

"In an old house in Paris that was covered in vines," I began, opening the book I actually knew by heart. I checked to see if Amanda was listening. She was, so I started to continue to tell the story: "... lived twelve little girls in two straight lines."

"Let's look out the window and see if somebody is coming," said Amanda, jumping up and dashing over to the window.

"How could they be coming if they can't drive to us?" I asked, closing the book. I thought I remembered the sound of a helicopter in my dreams, but I wasn't sure. "Maybe they could pick us up in a helicopter like they do on TV," I said to myself as much as to Amanda.

"Yeah! That would be fun. Right, Bear?" answered Amanda, who was trying to console her bear.

Bear nodded her head.

The morning dragged by and the afternoon was eternal. Sleep intervened for relief and dreams, and books saved us from our secret fears and the boredom that was intense.

Where were Mom and Dad? Why didn't they come home? Should we keep waiting? Shouldn't we do something besides just sit there?

Our Boat

Twenty long, scary, lonely hours had passed since our parents had left, and there was still no sign of them. The phone was dead and the electricity was still off.

I couldn't help groaning as I looked down from the top of the stairs at the water that was taking over inside our house. I could see a bunch of things floating around on the surface, like an apple core and some orange peelings, and my homework!

"Amanda, come and look at our living room! It's a swimming pool! Get on your bathing suit!" I kidded, even though I really felt pretty sick to see what was happening. Actually, we were wearing sweaters by now.

"Wow, all our stuff is floating around down there! Look! Here's Mommy's favorite lampshade!" said Amanda.

We ran back to the window again and looked out and saw that the water had risen so quickly that we couldn't even see a lot of our swing set.

I went back to the stairs and watched the plants and a Kleenex box floating in the hallway. Plastic spoons and paper plates were floating around in circles. The plastic wastebasket from the kitchen was bobbing around and there were banana peels and more orange peels and bits of crumpled paper bobbing around in the water.

Tears rolled down my cheeks, and I turned away whenever I thought Amanda was looking. In the sheer frustration of loneliness, boredom, curiosity, sadness, fear and worry, I decided that it was time to do something. Waiting and waiting was no longer the answer. Nobody had come. I realized we needed to escape. I wondered how.

Then I remembered our red rowboat, which was in the garage. It was small for a rowboat, and lightweight. I was pretty sure I could get it down from the garage wall, even though it would be very heavy for me. I remembered watching Dad take it down. Maybe I could do it—I thought I could. Finally I decided I would try to get it down and row it to the Community Center with Amanda and find our mommy and daddy.

Rain

The rain beat against our upstairs bedroom windows. I could hear the water sloshing and lapping against the inside walls of our living room! My heart thumped so hard someone could have heard it echoing through the valley as far as the distant hills past Sacramento.

I glanced back at my sister Amanda napping on my bed. Her teddy bear lay wide-eyed, hugged by her small, clutching arm. As I tiptoed towards the staircase and looked down at the water from the flood of the Sacramento River swirling in our house on the first floor, I had the feeling I was about to descend Mount Everest, and then plunge into an ocean.

I took off my sweater and jeans and put them on the dry staircase, then pulled my socks and tennis shoes off and put them next to my clothes. I inched down the stairs towards the entry hall and slipped my feet into the cold, dark water. As I continued down the stairs to try to get our boat down from the garage, the freezing water tickled, bubble by bubble, up my body until it reached my neck and threatened my chattering teeth.

Upstairs Amanda woke up and started whimpering like a baby. Then came the yelling. "Where are you? Come back! Elizabeth, come back!"

"I'm coming in a minute," I yelled back to her firmly, walking through the water and pulling the freezing water alongside my body with my fingers joined like they were glued. "Just wait right there and don't move!" I yelled.

As I braved it through the dirty water in the living room toward the outside of the house by the back double doors, I felt like an elephant pushing its whole body against a giant tree, leaning its shoulder against the doors.

I pushed through the cluttered, muddy water, and I held my head high, dragged myself around the house and pushed myself over to the open garage door, managing to wade into the flooded garage. I aimed myself, like the Leaning Tower of Pisa, in the direction of our red rowboat hanging on the garage wall.

The water was rising so fast, I wondered if I would have to swim any minute.

The boat was beckoning me to use it for what I now considered to be the real reason Dad had bought it, though, of course, no one could have guessed it at the time.

I was determined to find our mom and dad. They were somewhere. They wouldn't just leave us alone all night unless they were in big trouble!

I had to find them, no matter what it would take to find out why they hadn't come home the night before.

Decisions

Our red boat was hanging by hooks on the wall. I looked up at it and was alarmed by how big it suddenly seemed. It had always appeared small when Daddy took it down from the hooks.

I glared and squinted down into the water. Bending my head forward so my chin was touching my chest, I searched for my father's three-foot ladder. Spotting it, I reached my hands towards it and grabbed it, dragging it through the water over to the wall. Even though it was under the water, I put one foot on the first rung. Then I climbed slowly to the top step, and grabbed at the wall to steady myself. I stood up gingerly, hoping the short ladder wouldn't fall over.

My feet were still under the water, and I slowly straightened my body up like a child who has reached the top of a mountain. I raised my arms really carefully towards the rowboat. The water was swirling around my feet on the top step of the ladder.

As I scanned the garage over my shoulder, I saw a garden glove and an empty plastic water bottle float by. There were cardboard boxes and bottles and newspapers floating around like little barges out at sea. They looked like miniature furniture to me.

When I looked back up at the boat, a pang of loneliness gripped my heart. I tried to push away a burning feeling in my tightening throat and wondered a little if I were strong enough to get that boat down and save our lives.

I could feel more tears falling down my cold cheeks, mingling with the flood's water drops, and I wished that my mommy and daddy were there to tell me what to do. But underneath the surface of my cold skin I could feel a hot rush of blood pounding through my veins. All I knew was that, even if I were only eleven years old, I had to get that boat down and push it through the water, climb in it and row it through the back doors and into the house. I had to find Mommy and Daddy. I dreaded the next move.

My fingers touched the edge of the boat. For a moment I had a horrible vision of the boat crashing down onto my head and knocking me out. I realized that if this happened, I would never be able save Amanda. I started to push and pull the boat. I stopped.

I thought about it one more time. My plan could be so dangerous if it went wrong. But then I was frightened that we would eventually end up on the rooftop with the water swirling higher and higher around us and with no boat to save us.

I realized again that even if they wanted to, my parents would not be able to get to us through the deep water in their car. So I kept pushing and pulling the boat, up and down, around and around. Little by little, our red boat shifted towards the edge of the hooks.

As I looked up at the boat, hovering there between hanging and falling, I choked back my tears and dread. I could feel my mouth curving downwards as a surge of resentment surfaced that *I* had to move this huge thing all by myself. Then somehow my courage took hold of my sadness and fear, and I gave one more really powerful push with the whole force of my body. I heard the scratching of the boat moving off its hooks and saw it sliding right towards me.

Amazed

Without thinking, I fell over sideways away from the approaching boat, like a tree falling after the shout of *"timber!"* from the short, submerged ladder into the dirty, cold water. The boat bumped a box full of tools, banged into a shovel handle, and landed with a thud and a splash.

I was breathing quickly and I knew my heart was thumping as hard and fast as a frightened rabbit's. Wiping my chin, I glanced at my hand and saw that it was a little bit bloody. To me, after the initial shock, it was a smear of courage and daring. I thought it was bloody with the redness of my desperation, trying to do the impossible. I wiped my chin again and stared at the fresh blood. My chin must have gotten banged when I jumped, but I really didn't even feel it.

As I looked up from my bloody hand I saw the sides of the red boat floating towards me.

The rim of the boat bounced before me and beckoned me to grab it. As I did, I think I cocked my head and raised my brown eyebrows and smiled, kind of amazed that I had got it down.

As I pushed and pulled the boat along through the murky water, my feet were hardly touching the floor. The cold water was now over four feet from the

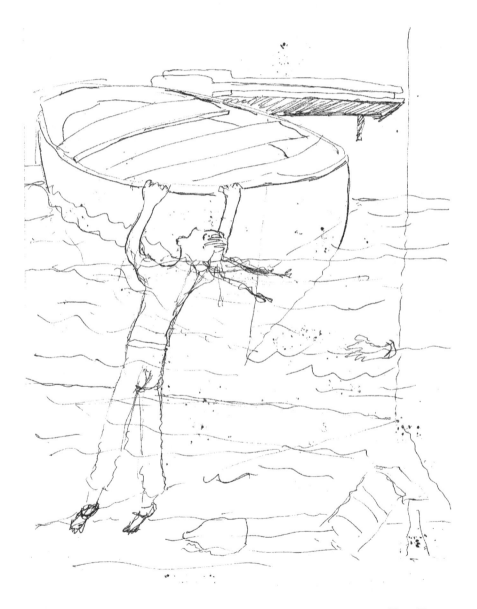

THE FLOOD

bottom floor of our house. It was up to my chin and I was afraid it would be up to my mouth if I didn't hurry. But I could only move through the water slowly, like a turtle on land with a full stomach, just touching the bottom with the tips of my toes.

I really wanted to have a closer neighbor that I could yell to for help, someone older and wiser, who could predict the future and maybe tell me about floods of long ago—somebody who could help me.

"Elizabeth, I'm coming to find you!" yelled Amanda from the bedroom window.

"No, you have to stay there! I'm coming right now! Amanda, you have to stay there! Please stay there!" I begged in my loudest, firmest and most parent-like voice.

"I'm going to count to ten and you better be here by then," yelled Amanda, mocking what I usually said to her.

"Count slowly!" I murmured to myself, and then loudly, "I'm coming!"

I willed myself to push the boat along so I could climb into it from the other ladder hanging on the wall on the other side of the garage. Then I could get in it and row out of the garage.

I lifted two oars from a shelf and tossed them into the boat one by one, making two loud thuds.

Then I spied a small, lightweight blue plastic tarp that was nearby on a shelf and grabbed it and slung it into the boat. I was alarmed to see that the water was now rising up past my chin, even though I was on tiptoes.

If I could just climb up the long, vertical ladder on the other side of the garage, I could step into the boat. I was determined to rescue Amanda. A new, strange combination of fear and confidence was carrying me along.

I finally pushed the boat across the garage and over to the long ladder, slurping the dirty water into my mouth sometimes, and spitting it out in disgust.

With the rope that was always tied onto the very front of the boat, I tied the boat to the ladder. I pulled the boat close to me as I climbed up the ladder. I put one of my soaking legs into our rowboat, pulling it closer to me with my foot. I held the ladder with one hand, and leaned down and put one foot into the boat, then threw my whole body into the boat, bumping my chin again.

"Elizabeth, where are you?" screamed Amanda again from upstairs.

"I'm getting the boat, Amanda. Stay exactly where you are! I'm coming!" I yelled back as loudly as I could, trying to sound confident.

"Well, hurry up! I counted to ten three times already. I'm scared!" she cried back to me.

I wiped a tear from my freezing cheek and wished hard, secretly, for my daddy to help me, to tell me what to do next. I felt my chin again where I had bumped it, and I saw that it was bleeding even more. I got up and sat down in the middle seat.

Because I remembered that sitting backwards was how to sit when you row a boat, I sat on the middle bench with my back facing the front! I grabbed the oars and put each one into its oarlock.

I tried to remember how to row. I knew the oars had to go around and around, but at first I made the boat go backwards. Then I remembered that I was the one who had to go backwards, while the boat went forwards. With a lot of splashing and mumbling, I started to row properly and managed to get over near the open garage door.

The water seemed to have risen even more since I had begun to get the boat down, and I could see I would have to duck to get through the doorway.

Struggling with the large oars, I tried to make them go the way I wanted them to, and I kept bumping into the wall. But somehow, while the boat shifted forwards and backwards, I managed to get through the garage opening. As I worked with the oars, I remembered the times at the lake with Dad and how I learned to row there. It was a very different scene, with the sun shining and Dad yelling encouragement. I sure missed him at that moment, but I was too busy even to cry.

While the rain beat against my face, I rowed around the house into the back yard and up to the French doors with a feeling of quiet pride. I gradually managed to open them wider as the boat lurched up and down and the water swished and bubbled.

Rowing into the House

I rowed into the house through the double door-way, bumping the oars and the sides of the boat against everything as I went. Reaching out with my hand, I guided the boat by pushing at the doorjamb when the boat was at its widest part in the doorway. I rowed past the tops of the tall dining room chairs bobbing by our grandfather clock, which was standing against the wall. It was still ticking, but I never noticed the time. I was too busy trying to row through the hallway and push the boat away from the walls, inching towards the half-submerged staircase.

On the way to the staircase, I remembered the food my mother had kept in one of the top shelves in the kitchen. I knew I could reach it from the boat now as the water was so high, and I thought that we might need some more food.

"Amanda, I am just getting some food!"

"No! You have to come here!"

"I can't. I will be right back in one minute!"

THE FLOOD

"One minute!" commanded Amanda. "I'm counting: one-a-thousand, two-a-thousand ..."

I moved the boat around with just one oar, pulling it towards my chest and pushing it away from me again. With the boat pointed in the direction of the cupboards, I rowed over and reached up and opened the cupboard doors. I stood up slowly, holding onto the shelf, and put one foot up onto the counter and then the other.

The boat moved away from me and bobbed around across the kitchen. I groaned. I looked around and saw the broom floating within arm's length. I reached for it. It was an inch too far away. I leaned harder towards it, but I started to fall into the water. I grabbed the cupboard handle just in time. I leaned over and used my hands to pull the water towards me, coaxing the broom closer. At last, I curled my fingers around it, and clutched it in my hand. Then I reached out with it towards the boat and hooked its straw shoulder onto the edge of the boat and gently pulled it back towards me.

I spied the candy bars and peanuts. Putting the broom down into the water, I leaned over, holding onto the cupboard handle, and slid my fingers around the rope on the front of the boat, and sighed with relief as I pulled it towards me.

I put my foot on top of the rope on the counter, then stood up carefully, anchored my foot on it, and grabbed the candy bars and peanuts. There were two heavy plastic one-gallon water containers my mom had kept up there for an emergency.

I heaved one off the shelf. It flew down into the boat jerking my shoulder and carrying me with it, and I almost fell as I let its weight pull my arm downward to the bottom of the boat. I let it go and it fell with such force that I thought it might put a hole in the bottom of the boat. But the boat was aluminum, so I was relieved to see that the worst it could do was make a dent. I was more careful with the second bottle, which I managed to lower into the boat with tenderness and respect no other bottle of water ever received!

I felt around the back of the shelf, picked up the flashlight my mother had kept there, and checked to see if it worked. It did, so I took it, too.

"What a great mom!" I said to the flashlight.

Then I climbed carefully back into the boat as it bobbed about, sat down slowly, rowed back through the kitchen door and over to the dry top half of the stairs. Holding the wooden banister, I climbed out of the boat onto a stair and tied up the boat to the banister, like a cowgirl tying up my horse in town. Tired and wet, I climbed up the carpeted stairs like a soggy kitten.

"I'm here, Amanda!" I said proudly as I rounded the corner towards the bedroom.

Leaving

Amanda was sitting on her little chair, and she fell over sideways, chair and all, when I came into the room so soaking wet. I hugged my little sister and tried to comfort her as she cried softly to herself.

Amanda cried, "Elizabeth, Elizabeth!" into my ear, and then, "Yuck, you're wet!" and pushed me away.

Alongside Amanda's chair lay a banana peel and a brown apple core. Across Amanda's face was a tiny smudge of banana. One braid was undone, while the other one remained intact. I was wet to the very top of my head and freezing.

I kissed Amanda's forehead and then went over to my dresser, opened the drawers, and pulled out a warm, long-sleeved shirt. I ran back to the stairs and picked up my shoes, socks, jeans and sweater and ran back up. After I peeled off my wet underwear and drying myself, I put on my jeans, my white shirt, red sweater, socks and shoes and grabbed my coat and slipped it on. I stuffed the food into my backpack and slung it over my shoulder.

"Come on, we have to go, quick, quick," I told Amanda, as I pulled her by the hand through the bedroom door to the top of the stairs and showed her the rising water and our little rowboat waiting for us half way down the stairs.

"Where's Bear? I want Bear!" wailed Amanda.

"Come on, we have to go now!"

"No, I won't go without Bear!"

"All right," I said, and rushed back into the bedroom and grabbed Bear and then, after a moment of hesitation, I slid my own old, worn brown bear, Sheila, into my coat pocket.

"Now, let's go! It's getting worse," I said, as I grabbed Amanda's cold hand. Amanda's eyes looked up at me. I knew she was depending on me and she believed I knew everything. I sure didn't feel like I did, but I wasn't going to disillusion her. I grabbed Amanda's coat.

"Put on your raincoat, Mandy," I told her.

She put it on right away, not asking for help. A little proud smile crept across Amanda's dirty face. I could see that, as she managed to put it on, there was a little smile of competence in the middle of her fear and sadness.

About halfway down the stairs the red rowboat was floating and I remembered when Daddy had bought it for us for our trips to Lake Rollins. We had had to flip a coin over the red one or the silver one, and I had won.

"Be careful, Mandy, it's slippery."

We climbed slowly down the stairs, trying not to slip on the wet places I had made climbing up, and held firmly onto the banister. I took Amanda's Bear and put it into my large coat pocket with Sheila, and I reached out to hold Amanda's hand.

Amanda had climbed into the boat many times before. She managed to climb into it quickly and swiftly with the assurance of a little mountain climber while it rocked from side to side. I took the two teddy bears out of my pocket, handed them to her, and tossed my backpack into the boat. As I crawled into the rocking boat, bending at my waist, I somehow avoided stepping on the food and water containers. After I untied the rope, I pushed the boat off from the stairs. I took a deep breath, and grabbed the oars.

"You can hold the bears while I row," I told Amanda, knowing that Amanda liked to feel helpful. I steadied the oars in the oarlocks, and rowed through our living room past the grandfather clock towards the partly opened double back doors. We would have to duck to get through them. We both lay down as flat as we could. The boat bumped into the doors and went back into the house.

We grabbed the doorjambs to pull ourselves through while we tried to shove the boat out of the doors. The boat bumped into the doors again, and since we had ducked down in the boat, we had missed our chance to grab the doorjambs again, so the boat bounced back into the house.

"Oh, no! The water must have gotten higher in the last few minutes!" I said. "I can't do it. Oh, heck. Ouch! I bumped my arm. Uh! Okay, Okay. We're going to try it again. Hold on, Amanda," I said, and took a big breath.

This time I pushed the top of the doorway up and the boat down with all my might. Amanda was lying as flat as she could and reaching out to the side of the door to help push the boat through. Finally, we just made it through.

"Whew! It was good we left when we did or we wouldn't have gotten out at all! Look at how high the water is now!" I said.

"We did it!" said Amanda, glancing at me then looking down at all the soggy things in the water.

"Now we have to get going. This has taken so long, it's already afternoon!" I said, examining the lighter clouds near the top of the mountains where the sun was still shining behind the clouds.

As I started to row, I wondered for a minute if we really should leave. Leaving was hard for me because I didn't know what we were doing or exactly where we were going. Leaving meant the unknown, the mysterious, taking a chance, like jumping off a cliff that had no clear bottom. Leaving was pushing through an invisible door into nowhere that might turn out to be scarier than it was now. Leaving was a crisis in my mind, but a barrier we had to go through.

It wasn't raining now. I looked around to see the familiar things that I would have to leave. I could only see the top of our swing set and our plastic toys floating away. Beneath the cloudy sky the rooftops of houses poked up from the water in the distance, and looked like submarines or dragons.

The rooftops of the houses that were only one story high, were almost totally under water, and looked sort of like Chinese boats with their square sails shimmering along the surface of the water. I muttered to myself, "Should we stay? Would it be safer? Should we leave? Maybe there will be horrible risks in front of us that would be harder than just staying."

"What?" asked Amanda, an arm around each teddy bear.

"Oh, nothing, just thinking," I answered, as I drew in my breath, counted to ten and decided that we definitely should leave. I didn't want to spend another night in the house with the water rising. "Anyway," I mumbled, "we will be at the Community Center in a couple of hours."

"What?" asked Amanda again.

"Oh, nothing, just hoping you were keeping the teddy bears warm," I answered with a smile.

"Oh, I am. We're very cozy," said Amanda, cuddling them closer.

"Mommy and Daddy love me," I mumbled again to myself, "and they love Amanda, too. I know they would come to us if they could. Maybe they're in trouble. I want my mommy and daddy!"

"What?" asked Amanda.

"I said we are going to see our mommy and daddy," I answered lightly.

"I know!" said Amanda.

I felt a lump in my throat. I swallowed hard, and held back my tears.

"I'm going to be a big girl now and take care you, Amanda," I said. "We'll find them. We'll have to be brave, that's all." But why didn't they come home?

"Be brave," repeated Amanda. "I am being brave, Elizabeth."

"Yes, you are, Amanda. You are really being very brave," I encouraged my little sister. I wiped my eyes, and took in deep breaths as I tried to row the way Daddy had taught me.

It was sprinkling just a little now as I rowed along. I was pretty sure I would find Mommy and Daddy at the Community Center, which was about thirteen miles away, Mommy had once told me.

The Rescue

I was pretending to be strong like my dad while I rowed, and being kind like my mom when I talked to Amanda. It was hard for me to row the little boat even with such a small passenger. I was proud that we had managed to get the boat through the back doors, and glad the water had not been too high to do it.

My hands were cold and red and my feet were cold in spite of the dry socks. I could keep a good eye on Amanda who was sitting at the back of the little boat, as I was facing her. It still felt strange to sit backwards to row forwards.

"I'm thirsty," said Amanda.

"Take a little water, then, but not a lot. We don't know where we'll get more, and we can't drink this muddy water," I cautioned, as I pulled the oars forward, leaned backwards, and nodded at the murky water we could not drink.

Amanda could not open the bottle, so I stopped rowing and opened the bottle for her and held it for Amanda to sip from. I then took a sip myself, closed the top and put the bottle back down.

I scanned the horizon, just like Dad would do. Only this time, it wasn't just a fun day at the lake. I wiped the wet hair from my eyes, and could see the tops of the houses scattered along what used to be the country road, looking so bedraggled and empty. Where had everybody gone?

The sound of a girl crying pricked up my ears and my eyes followed my ears. The sound came from Maya's house. Squinting towards the top window, I saw my younger friend, Maya, sitting in an upstairs window crying.

"Hey! That's Maya-chan! Here we come," I yelled, and rowed as hard as I could towards her. I knew we could fit one more small child, who was now seven years old, into the boat, and I really liked Maya, too, so it was an easy decision to make.

"I want my mommy, where is my mommy? They said they would be right back!" she yelled. I could see she was crying quietly and trying to be brave.

"We're looking for our mommy, too. Come on, get in the boat and you can come with us!" I yelled again.

The top bedroom window was still a little high, but we could probably reach Maya.

As I rowed towards her, I heard a cat meow. I saw that Maya was now holding Ginny, her cat. Of course, we could fit a small black cat into the boat. But I knew that cats hated water—she would never jump out! So, very carefully, Maya handed Ginny down to me, and I handed her to Amanda, who cuddled her so cozily that Ginny started purring.

Then Maya handed me a box of cookies, a loaf of bread, and a package of butter. The boat was beginning to look quite full. Then Maya handed me her raincoat, and I gave it to Amanda who held it over Ginny.

Maya was slightly built, and she was very athletic for her age. Under her black bangs, though, her face showed that she looked a little frightened. Carefully she put first one foot over the windowsill, and then the other foot, slid a little bit downwards and rested her feet on the seat of the boat. She was still holding onto the windowsill while standing up in the rocking boat. I helped Maya with my free hand as she squatted down onto the seat. The boat rocked so I sat right back down as well.

Now we were all safely in the boat. As I pushed my hair out of my eyes, Maya pushed her bangs away from her eyes at the same time. We laughed and looked into each other's faces with a new understanding of what friendship means, and we were ready to be on our way.

Three Girls and a Cat

Somewhere in the distance a dog barked, but we didn't know where, and we didn't have room anyway. I remembered that some dogs liked water, and also that they all could swim without any lessons!

I rowed for a long time in the direction of the town. The boat seemed heavier now with Maya and a cat and all our food in it. My arms began ache, and I was breathing very hard. It was fternoon when I looked up and saw that the re almost dark. The rain was very slight etting colder. I was glad we were r warm coats.

into a tree. Wiping my hair at my three charges and dy to help us soon. at and just let it bottled water somewhere. It be no grownups ny chest was a new

en
nd
other
dy do,
distant
extremely
cat. Maya
e that I was
lizabeth, did
?"

THE FLOOD

kind of ache, an exhilaration of danger and fear and the unknown, all banging around together, making my stomach do roller coaster lunges.

What happened to our parents, I wondered to myself? Maybe we will see them coming in a motorboat to the house to save us, I thought. Maybe they are in the flood, too, and trying to get to us. Maybe we should have stayed home. But nobody had come to our aid, even though we were stranded overnight and a long morning. It was altogether too quiet, except for that helicopter I thought I had heard the evening before.

Now there were just clouds and rain, a small boat, a cat and the three of us girls.

Suddenly I noticed we were drifting westwards, which I had thought was in the direction of the town, but now I realized I needed to row the other way. The town was east, and I had gott confused. I sighed, and turned the boat aro using one paddle pushing one way, and the pulling the other way as I had seen my da and started rowing in the direction of the hills. I rowed and rowed and was feeling tired, pulling the three of us and the was a sympathetic child, who could se having a little trouble, so she said, "I you know that I can row a boat, to

"Oh, that's good, 'cause I am getting tired," I answered. "Come and sit by me and take one oar, and let's see if we can row together."

Half bent over so that she would not rock the boat too much, Maya stepped forward and slid into a place I made next to me on the seat. Maya took one of the oars, made sure it was well into its oarlock, and we started to count so we would keep rowing in time together.

"One, two, three, ROW, one, two, three, ROW, one, two, three, ROW," we chanted, as we dipped our oars into the water at the same time, and pulled them up and out into the air, and plunged them in again to pull the boat along. We started moving faster.

"Watch out for that tree," yelled Amanda whose sharp eyes caught sight of it in spite of the growing darkness, just in time. We dodged it by raising our oars into the boat, and leaning away from it.

But as hard as we rowed, we never seemed to get any nearer to the Community Center. It looked like we were moving pretty well, but when I could just make out a familiar tree I had once climbed, I knew that we were hardly moving at all. It was getting much darker and Amanda was shivering.

Somewhere to Sleep

"**M**aybe we won't make it to the Community Center today," I said, trying not to sound too discouraged. "Maybe we will have to stay in one of the empty houses."

I looked behind us in the direction we were rowing, and saw the upper story of a house we had run by many times before. We didn't know who lived there, but I thought we would see if any upstairs windows were open. We rowed as hard as we could, and in about another half an hour, we were quite close to it.

The water here was higher than it was at our house, so we could easily row right up to the upstairs window. I looked up at the house now and wondered if we should be trying to get into a stranger's house. It looked haunted with no lights on, but there didn't seem to be much choice.

"The window's open a little bit. Let's try to climb in," I said, excitedly. I brushed my hair out of my eyes, and felt a little like I was finding my mother.

Of course, I wasn't, but it was a relief to be doing something other than just rowing!

We pushed the boat right next to the house, and then rowed along the side of the house until we were by the open window. I slowly stood up, and, on my toes, I held onto the windowsill with one hand, and put the fingers of my other hand underneath the window which was only an inch open, and pushed the window up.

"Helloooooo?" I yelled. Then all three of us yelled, "helloooooo?" But there was no answer.

"I'll climb in and see if we can stay here," I told the girls. With the little rope on the bow of the boat, I tied it to a pipe next to the window. I grabbed the flashlight. Maya held the wall so we would not move away from the house. I set the flashlight onto the window ledge, held the ledge with both hands, and peeked into the room. I couldn't see much, so I held tightly with one hand, reached for the flashlight with the other hand, turned it on and pointed it into the room.

"Wow! You should see what is in here!" I said to the girls.

Swim, Amanda, Swim!

I dropped the flashlight onto the floor and heaved myself up on top of the windowsill. I swung one leg over it and then the other leg and launched myself right into the room, slipping headfirst down to the floor onto my side.

I picked up the flashlight and turned it on, checking the room.

"Wow!" I said, my eyes widening, my brain whirling.

Amanda stood up in the boat to see and the boat started to rock. Amanda grabbed onto Maya who had just stood up, too, and both Maya and Amanda lost their balance and the boat almost flipped over. Both of the girls tumbled into the water like two acrobats.

"Help! Help!" yelled Amanda. I looked out the window with the flashlight and nobody was in the boat! I saw the top of Amanda's head just going under the water. It came up again, and Amanda's hands splashed around in front of her as she came up for air.

"Swim, Amanda, swim! You know how! Swim," I shouted, ready to jump in after her, but not liking the idea of the cold water. Amanda's head stayed above the water now, and she moved her arms and hands sideways to tread water. I saw in an instant that she remembered to close her fingers together to make webbed hands like a duck. I saw that Amanda would be okay until I could get over to her in the boat.

Maya was paddling towards Amanda to help her. Quickly, I pulled the rope and got the boat to the window. I was glad I had tied the boat to the pipe on the side of the house. Climbing out of the window and back into the boat, I was amazed at my own speed, as I tossed the flashlight onto the food. In spite of the growing darkness, with the moon shining through the clouds, I could just see the girls. I could reach them easily now. Crouching down, I stuck my hands out towards both of the girls and grabbed both at once.

"Hold on, hold on, I'm pulling you into the boat, it's okay," I said, but the two girls were surprisingly heavy for me and I was so tired from rowing. I led Maya's hand to the side of the boat as I pulled Amanda next to her, and yelled to them both. "Hold on tight to the boat! Hold on to the boat."

Maya grabbed the side of the boat with one hand, and then with the other. She spit out the muddy water that had gotten into her mouth. Even though the boat was rocking, I managed to grab Amanda's other hand, and pulled her to the boat's edge, too, and said, "Hold onto the boat, Amanda," and Amanda, spluttering and breathing hard, did just that.

"Can you climb into the boat?" I asked them both, exhausted myself.

"I'll try," said Maya, who made an effort that only rocked the boat more violently. Amanda lost her grip with one hand and I grabbed her arm, which was flailing about. I put her hand back onto the boat's side and pressed her fingers around it.

"Now, hold on tight with both hands, Amanda. Maya, you have to come around to the other side of the boat and hold it down while I pull Amanda in. Otherwise we might tip over. Come over here," I patted the other side of the boat.

The bow of the boat was securely fastened by the rope, which was holding well. Tied to the front of the pipe, each side was free and away from the house, while the front of the boat pointed at the house. Maya moved her hands, one over the other, slowly around the back of the boat and around to the other side. Her teeth were starting to chatter.

"I want my mommy," cried Amanda.

"Look, Amanda, just try to let me pull you into the boat, okay?" I asked as sweetly as I could under the circumstances. I wiped my hands on my wet clothes to get them cleaner, and then I grabbed Amanda's arms, and I said in a firm, rather loud voice, "Okay, Amanda, let go with this hand, but hold onto the boat with that hand until I get you in. Now start kicking really hard!"

I pulled Amanda with all my might, and it was much harder than I thought it would be. I pulled and pulled and leaned back so my hair was almost in Maya's mouth on the other side. I couldn't believe how heavy Amanda was.

Amanda, a climber from way back when she was a baby, heaved her little leg over the side of the boat, and with my help moved up onto her stomach and rolled over into the boat on top of all the food.

"Good, Amanda, good girl. What a climber!" I told her, turning around right away to help Maya. Ginny was still just sitting there in the boat, almost unaware of the trouble we were having. But she was watching closely with wide eyes and delicately balancing as the boat rocked up and down. Amanda recovered and tried to help Maya, too, but it was much harder because Maya seemed so heavy.

"Take your coat off and give it to me," I said to Maya. Maya managed to get one arm free with mumbling and protests, and then the other arm with my help. I grabbed Maya's coat and tossed it into the boat, then grabbed one of her arms, and

Maya tried to heave herself up onto the boat while we pulled her towards us.

She also swung one leg onto the side of the boat, and Amanda caught it and held it with the toughness of a dog pulling a stick. Maya was strong, and with much groaning and moaning from all three of us, Maya heaved her body into the boat onto her stomach, accidentally kicking poor Amanda in the shoulder. Amanda didn't even cry, she was so glad that Maya was saved. All of us were shivering and panting and breathless, and we were so relieved that we started to laugh!

"We did it, we did it!" I yelled, picking up Ginny and handing her to Amanda. I laughed, thrilled that we had accomplished something that the day before would have seemed impossible.

The Food

"I'm cold. I'm soaking wet! Let's get into the house. Anyway, what's in the room?" asked Maya, her teeth chattering.

"Oh, yes, come on, let's get in there," I said with a smile.

Very, *very* carefully, I helped Amanda into the window, and then Maya and Ginny. I heaved myself up onto the windowsill and swung one leg over and then the other leg. A second later I was in the room.

Our food was in its plastic bags in the boat, but it didn't matter because the room we climbed into had food all over the dresser and a table. It had a large, unopened bag of sugar, and powdered milk and peanut butter and a jar of jelly. It had crackers and bottled water and peanuts in large jars. It had dozens of fig bars and boxes of graham crackers. There was salt and olive oil. There was enough soap and detergent to wash our whole schools' dirty clothes. She even thought of paper towels and toilet paper, and two fat candles and a

THE FLOOD

large box of matches. Whoever lived in this house was very nice.

We were all very hungry. Opening the peanut butter and the jelly jars, and then the crackers, I spread the peanut butter onto the crackers with my finger. I passed out two crackers to each girl and gave two to myself, then poured the jelly onto it. I shivered and told them to take off their wet clothes as soon as they ate.

We ate greedily and happily. Ginny licked my peanut-buttered finger. I drank a bit of water, then put powdered milk into the water bottle we found there, and shook it until it was a bubbly milky drink, and we all had many gulps which made the peanut butter wash away from the roofs of our mouths and our sticky teeth.

I stood the red candles up in their holders on the dresser, took the large box of matches, and looked at the girls. My father had told me not to use matches, but he had also taught me how to strike a match and make a campfire when we camped by the lake. So, even though I knew I wasn't supposed to, I struck the match, making sure I struck it away from my body. It glowed brightly while Amanda and Maya watched, spellbound. I lit the two candles, and shook the lighted match, as I had seen my father do. It was almost like a birthday party! We all clapped as the room lit up. It seemed to make us feel warmer.

With darkness creeping across the whole sky, and the light of the day now quite gone, we decided we had better spend the night right there even though it was so cold. We could get an early start in the morning rowing towards the Community Center, which, hopefully, was not further away than a mile.

We peeled off our muddy, wet clothes, and went into the bedroom closet and found huge slippers that I put on. Amanda opened a drawer and pulled out two grown-up sized T-shirts, and she and Maya put them on. The shirts went down to their ankles, and they looked like two monkeys all dressed up. Maya giggled. I was still dry enough that I didn't need to change my clothes. Then all three of us fell into the large double bed and wrapped our legs and arms around each other to keep warm, and I blew out the candles and we tried to go to sleep.

"I can't sleep," said Amanda.

"Then be quiet, so we can," I answered.

"It's dark and I'm scared," said Amanda.

"Let's tell a story," said Maya. She said she always made her parents tell her stories at bedtime.

"You tell us a story, then, 'cause I'm too tired," I said.

"Well, okay," said Maya, and she began.

"Once upon a time, there were three children who were lost in a flood and looking for their mommies and daddies ... and they had to row really hard and they couldn't get to the Community Center, so they found a house with lots of food in it, and fell into the water from the boat, but ended up safe and sound in the big bed. The End."

"Is that all?" asked Amanda.

"Yes, I am too tired to think of anything else. Oh, yes, and they had a cat who was a good swimmer, but didn't like the water, and she kept them good company in their trials, and liked very much to cuddle with them in the big bed. The End."

"That was better," I said, as I turned over, yawned, and tried to go to sleep.

"Do another one," I heard Amanda pleading.

"You do it, I'm too tired, but I will listen," replied Maya.

"Once upon a time, there was a cat," began Amanda. "It was a beautiful black cat. There was also a little girl who loved the cat. One day the cat climbed high into a tree and got stuck, and the little girl had to climb the tree to save her. She was very scared, but she loved her cat, so she started to climb and climb up the tree. Are you listening, Maya?" she asked.

But Maya had fallen asleep, so Amanda said, "So she climbed the tree, scraped her knee, and got her kitty down, safe and sound. The End. Hey, that rhymes!"

Soon Amanda fell off to sleep, and the bed stopped moving and wiggling, and I could just faintly hear the sound of the rain upon the water outside as my eyes closed, taking me into another land.

My Dream

In my dream that night, I was in another boat that was like a canoe. The water was salty in my mouth as the waves crashed around my boat and me and I lunged into the bottom of a wave and up to the top of the next. I was younger in the dream, and I kept looking for land every time the boat crested a wave. My hand was placed almost permanently above my eyebrows to keep the sunlight out of my eyes.

Sometimes the boat went straight off the top of the wave and flew for miles while I scanned the horizon. Then I would find myself at the bottom of a trough again on the way up for a repeat of the searching look and my horrible disappointment as the boat tipped over the white foam and headed downwards again.

A dolphin swam by and said, "Don't worry, I will lead you home if you can't find the way." And then the dolphin disappeared and did not return. Was I going to be stuck in the same routine forever?

A whale swam nearby and talked with a deep voice like my father's.

"Don't worry," he said softly, "If you can't find land, I will lead you there." Just as I started to smile in relief, the whale submerged its huge, shiny, gray body and the ocean looked deserted.

An albatross flew above me and came to land on the bow of my boat.

"Hey," I yelled. "You're tipping my boat over. Go away."

So the albatross lifted his enormous wings, flapped his wet feathers in my face, circled high above me and then swooped down and said, "If you can't find the land, I will help you," and then he disappeared forever behind the next mountain of water. I never found out if any of them would have come back because just then my dream was interrupted.

I woke up, thinking I heard a strange noise. I sat up in bed, moving Amanda's leg, which was wrapped around my own. The blankets were off the bed, so I pulled them up again and spread them over the sleeping girls and the cat.

It had stopped raining. I crept out of bed and went over to the window and looked out. The boat was there, moving silently back and forth. The moon was quite full and I could see the trees and the rooftops in the distance. I wondered if anybody might be in the house. We were so tired when we arrived that we had fallen asleep in the double bed almost as soon as we had eaten.

I lit the candle, again being sure to strike the match away from my body, and went over to the bedroom door. I tiptoed out by the bathroom, which we had used just before going to sleep. The toilet didn't flush for some reason, and it was smelly in there, but we used it anyway.

Softly padding past another door, I stopped to listen. I heard a noise behind me. It was a slight thud. My heart began to beat against my chest as hard as a drum. Then silence. I listened and stood quite still. Then I felt a warm, furry feeling on my leg, which startled me, and then I realized that the noise was just Ginny who must have knocked a shoe down from the bed when she jumped off. I picked her up and petted her. Ginny purred. I turned around and walked back into the bedroom, put Ginny onto the bed, and then walked out again, this time closing the door behind me. It creaked.

Again, I listened. It was very quiet. I tiptoed towards another door on the upper floor that was closed. Putting my hand on the handle, I turned it as quietly as anyone could, and gently pushed the door open.

It was dark in spite of the candle, and I could not see much except the outline of a bed and a dresser and two lamps on two small tables. I started to breathe hard, so I just stood there and waited until I calmed down. My ears ached from listening for someone breathing or any other noise.

The darkness scared me and I couldn't tell what those shapes on the other side of the room were with just the candlelight. I was not afraid of monsters anymore, most of the time. It was very quiet. It didn't feel like anyone was there. I walked in. The candlelight was just enough light to see that it was just another bedroom, but this one didn't have any food in it! I decided I would have a quick look in the morning to see it better, before we left in our boat again.

Retracing my footsteps back into the other bedroom, I grabbed some peanuts, climbed back into the bed, and sat up, thinking about what to do tomorrow.

Soon, I finished the peanuts, blew out the candle, yawned a very wide yawn, and slid back down into a deep slumber.

A Hungry Cat

Later on in the night, I woke up and my eyes opened a tiny bit, as I thought I heard another noise. I could just make out that Ginny had gone to sit at the closed window, maybe to see what was happening in the tree.

Ginny was probably hungry, and I wondered if she were hoping to catch a bird. But there were no birds in the tree. Ginny obviously didn't like peanuts, and the peanut butter Amanda tried to feed her had probably stuck to the roof of her mouth, and there wasn't any cat food around, as hard as Ginny seemed to be sniffing around for it.

I kept peeking out of the covers at Ginny sitting by the window. She was hunched up with her tail twitching.

Just then, a little mouse ran speedily across the room, like it was on motorized skates. I cringed, but watched it quietly. Ginny crouched down, her ears pointing up high, and looked like she was listening intensely for a hint of where the mouse had gone.

Ginny's eyes looked huge to me in the moonlight and I realized that she could see quite well even though it was pretty dark. Ginny saw the mouse again in the corner of the room. She flicked her tail. Crouching down, her eyes never left the mouse. Her tail twitched again as her body crept dangerously closer. She stopped and stayed as still as a lioness, ready to pounce on her kill.

The full moon went behind a cloud and then came out and it was bright and shining onto the floor. The silence was total. Ginny looked ready to charge. I imagined that she was very hungry.

It happened so quickly; it must have been when I blinked. One second she was on the windowsill and the next her mouth and claws had pinned the mouse down on the floor. Within minutes, she ate the mouse and chewed the bones, making horrible crunching noises. I didn't think I could ever pet her again.

She jumped back onto the windowsill and cleaned her paws and her white whiskers with her pink tongue and licked her whole body, making her black fur smooth and soft.

Jumping down onto the floor, she walked softly over to the bed, sprung up onto it, and lay down next to Amanda's warm body. She curled up and closed her eyes, and I could hear a faint purring sound.

I closed my eyes and wondered if I had just had a dream. In a few moments, I knew that they were all sleeping, even Ginny, and my eyelids were closing heavily, ready to be back in the land of dreams.

The Next Morning

The next morning the sun finally came up and it was heaven for us to see a little blue in the cloudy sky. Things almost began to feel normal to us.

Our boat was half full of water from more rain, so I pulled it by its rope up to the window and grabbed all the things we had left in it. I pulled the boat sideways, grunting as I tried to lift it up to get some of the water out that was in it. But I put it back down again, as it was too heavy. I could get some out with the bucket Dad had tied to it. I climbed in and worked hard at pouring out some of the water with the bucket. I tossed the rest of the food into the window and got back in. Some of it was a bit wet, but we would still be able to eat it.

The girls were still sleeping, so I went for a quick trip back to the other bedroom, and found it a little more colorful than in the middle of the night, with bedspreads of beautifully colored roses. I noticed a piece of paper on one bed, so I went over and read it.

It said: "To anyone who finds this note: In the other bedroom there is some food I always keep on hand for emergencies. Please help yourself and you can live here if you want to until I return. I am being flown in a helicopter to dry land, but I want anyone who might be stuck to feel free to stay here if they need to. Yours sincerely, Mrs. Hendricks."

I felt very much taken care of by this unknown person, Mrs. Hendricks, and it warmed me to think that, in a way, a grown-up was looking after us.

I smiled and went back into our bedroom to wake the girls.

"Come on, you two, we have to go," I said as I jiggled their bodies gently.

"I want my mommy," said Amanda first thing, hugging her bear.

"I want my mommy, too," I said back to Amanda. "That's why we have to get up. We have to find them and we might even have to help them."

At this, Maya sat straight up, her penetrating young eyes looking into the distance.

"Will I have to help my mother? How strange," she mumbled and slumped back down and fell deep in thought for a minute. Then she cocked her chin sideways and upwards with a serious expression on her face. "I'm hungry!"

"Have some peanut butter on crackers, here," I said, and Maya helped open the jars while I opened the crackers. We mixed powered milk into the water and poured it into the paper cups we found there. Ginny got some milk, too.

"I found a note from the lady who lives here," I said. "It says anybody who finds the food can eat it and stay here as long as they need to, until she gets back. Imagine that! Thinking about somebody else just when a helicopter is taking you away. She was some planner, wasn't she?"

"Yeah, and I am sure glad about that! How come a helicopter didn't rescue us?" asked Maya, her mouth full of crackers and peanut butter and jelly, which she said was her favorite combination. Ginny licked a little peanut butter off Maya's cheek.

"I don't know. Do you think we should stay here, or do you think we should go?" I asked, mostly to myself.

"We should go! We want to find Mommy and Daddy!" said Amanda. Maya nodded with her mouth full, and made um-huh noises.

"Okay, eat, go to the bathroom, put your clothes on, which are still probably pretty wet, and then we will put the food in the boat and go. Thank goodness it's sunny!" I said, picking up a bottle of water and walking over to the window. "Maybe a helicopter will come and find us, too."

Goodbye Nice House

I held the rope that was connected to the bow of the boat while standing in the window, and pulled the boat alongside of the house. Maya carefully climbed over the windowsill and back into the boat. It rocked up and down, but Maya was getting used to how the boat moved, and getting much better at staying balanced.

"Hey, me, me," begged Amanda, her hands outstretched.

"Hold on, let's get Maya seated first, then I can help you and kitty down," I answered.

"Oh! Oh! It's rocking! But I can sit down," said Maya. She finally sat down, looked up at me and said, "Okay, hand me some stuff."

"No, me, me first," yelled Amanda.

"Oh, all right," I said, and Maya and I helped Amanda down into the rocking boat.

"Now, go carefully, Amanda, and sit on the back seat, okay?" I said.

"Okay. But I need Ginny, too."

"First sit down, then I will hand Ginny to you," said Maya.

Amanda stayed low as she reached towards the bench at the back of the boat and sat down. I found Ginny next to my leg, picked her up and handed her to Maya, who handed her to Amanda who was holding her hands up towards her.

"I want my Bear," said Amanda, not content with just Ginny.

"Here is your bear, and here is mine, too, so you be the babysitter, Amanda, okay?" I said.

I handed down three small plastic bags of the food we had found in the house, and also a small blanket and a sheet. I could sit on it while I rowed. Maya grabbed each bag and somehow found a place on the floor under her bench to stow each one, and then sat next to Amanda.

"Goodbye nice house," I said as I flung one foot over the windowsill, looking back once to see if we had forgotten anything.

Carefully I lowered myself into the boat while the girls held onto the sides. It started rocking again. I held onto the windowsill as the boat moved. I pulled the boat closer to the house with my feet, then squatted down, grabbed the top edge of the boat with one hand, and let go of the windowsill.

I squatted down right away and sat in my place ready to row. We were still wearing the big shirts, but put our damp coats back on top.

The boat moved away from the house, but the rope was still tied to the pipe, so I pulled on the rope until the boat was near the pipe, and undid my knot. It was pretty tight and I had to pick at it, breaking my fingernail, and working hard at it, until the knot finally came undone. I brought the rope into the boat, hand over hand. It was wet. I tried to make a coil, as I had seen my daddy do, but it looked more like a wiggly snake.

I grabbed an oar, feeling quite experienced now. First I turned the boat around by paddling with one oar then I pushed our boat away from the house with my other oar and pointed it in the direction of the Community Center.

"Here we go. Hold on tight and in a while, Maya, you can come and help me," I said.

"Okay," answered Maya.

"Meow. Meow," said Ginny, who had perfect balance, and did not need to hold onto the boat. I looked behind myself now and again to see where I was rowing, then looked at my little sister who had reached for Ginny so she could cuddle her, and then at Maya who was tidying the food bags.

The water seemed to be dragging us backwards, like there was a current fighting us with every stroke of our oars. As I looked at Maya and Amanda, I noticed just how dirty they were and that their hair was such a mess. Then I realized I must look just as messy, maybe even more. I brushed my hand across my forehead getting my hair out of my eyes, pulled hard on the oars, and hoped that we were making some progress in the direction of the Community Center.

The Helicopter

"I wonder where my mom is?" said Maya. "Do you think she is pretty upset, wondering where I am, too? I hope we can make it to the Community Center by tonight," she said, wiping her eye with the back of her hand.

"Yeah, it seems sort of strange that they haven't found us yet, but I am sure they are trying to," I said, trying to reassure the younger girls. "Maybe they don't have a boat. We do, thank goodness, so let's just keep going till we get to the Community Center and find them," I added, keeping up a good rowing pace all the while.

Amanda seemed to be in a little world of her own, holding Ginny, and whispering in her ear, "You don't have to worry. We'll take care of you." Amanda was looking into Ginny's ears, which were probably dirty inside. They were mostly black on the furry outside, with streaks of white sticking out from the inside. Her face was black but her whiskers were white. Her hair wasn't very long, but it was soft.

Amanda started picking a little mud off Ginny's feet. That started Ginny licking and cleaning, as if to help Amanda. Ginny stuck her rear foot right out and up to her little mouth, like an acrobat, and then cleaned her inside legs and all around her tail. Amanda held her gently so the movement of the boat wouldn't disturb her cleaning.

"I think we're actually getting somewhere today," I said, noticing we were now quite some distance from the house we had left earlier. As I didn't want to get lost, I followed where I thought the winding road was below us under the water. I had never before seen branches of these trees from so high up, so I couldn't really be sure about the road. It was too muddy to see the bottom. The branches of the trees either side were almost touching us. They sometimes touched each other, and we had to duck or go around. We saw a nest left from last spring. It went right by our noses. No baby birds were in it, though. There were clouds gathering in the distance, towards the town in the east.

"Oh, dear," I said, looking behind me. "I think it is going to rain again soon. Look at those black clouds." The girls looked ahead of them and looked at the clouds, and then Maya again fiddled with the bags and Amanda sang quietly.

"Maya, come and help me row. I'm tired," I said. Slowly Maya bent her body in half like an old man, and turned around, plopping down next to me as I slid over just in time.

"Take the oar," I said, and we started our routine: "One, two, three, ROW, one, two, three, ROW, one, two, three, ROW!"

Maya worked as hard as a sailor and after a while both of us were complaining about blisters that were starting to form on our hands.

"Let's tie up to a tree and have a rest," I said.

Amanda stopped singing. "Yes, and some food."

So we rowed over to some tree branches, which still had leaves on them. We rowed under them, and felt protected by their encircling arms. The branches were just the right height to tie up to. I made a firm knot called a bowline—the kind my dad had taught me to do. The boat swung around so that the higher branches made a little canopy over us.

It was peanut butter on crackers again, but with a dessert of fig bars, and some water to wash it all down.

"When will we be there?" asked Maya, licking her fingers.

"How should I know? Well, let's see: maybe in a few hours, maybe. I don't know. We seemed to be getting somewhere today, but if we have any trouble, I don't know," I answered, trying not to sound as concerned as I really was.

"Do you think my mommy is looking for me?" asked Maya.

"I think your mommy is looking for you, and our mommy is looking for us. I wonder if they tried to find us at our house somehow?" I pondered this and then said, "Hey, remember that helicopter noise that last night there? Do you think, maybe … it could have been looking for us or something? But it didn't stop, so maybe not."

"Hey, there's a helicopter over there above where the Community Center is," said Maya, pointing eastwards.

"Yeah, I think it is," I answered. "Hey, look, there's a person dangling below it. Hey, they're pulling him up to the helicopter. I wonder who he is and what's going on?" I squinted to see into the distance.

Getting Bigger!

Amanda stared at the helicopter. She said it looked just like a toy, a toy right in front of her in the sky. She even reached out and tried to touch it. She couldn't touch it, of course. She was acting as if it were just a little out of her reach.

"It has a doll hanging from it, a tiny human-looking doll. It's moving. There are two dolls in the toy helicopter that are moving, too," she exclaimed. "You guys, look. It's a toy helicopter!"

"No, silly, it's real," said Maya.

"It looks like a toy," said Amanda, cocking her head a little to imagine how it could possibly be real.

"Well, actually, it is far away from us," I said, remembering once when I was about four years old, seeing a distant train when we were in the car, and thinking it was a toy. Mom told me it was real, but I just couldn't believe it. I stared and stared at it and tried to make it far away in my head, but it still looked just like a toy that I could reach out and touch.

"It's coming this way, Amanda, now can you see it? It's getting bigger, see?" I said.

"It IS getting bigger! Look! It IS bigger!" exclaimed Amanda, her eyes getting bigger also.

The helicopter flew nearer, but not near enough to see us because we were just then hidden from the helicopter's view as we were under the branches. We started waving and yelling but the helicopter flew on past us.

"Hellooooo, help, hey, here we are, help!" we yelled as loudly as we possibly could.

"Oh, darn, darn, darn!" I said. "Maybe they saw us and will come back. Anyway, we have to keep going and find our mommies and daddies. Come on." Amanda started to cry.

"Hey, Amanda, maybe they'll come back. Don't worry. It's going to be okay. We can do this all by ourselves, anyway, right?" I said bravely, nodding my head.

Amanda sniffed and looked at me and nodded, too, wiping her tears away.

I figured we had rowed about seven miles from our house yesterday, then another four miles from the house where we slept, and still had about two miles to go to the Community Center. I untied the knot, started rowing again and we began to count and work up a now familiar rhythm:

"One, two, three, ROW, one, two, three, ROW, one, two, three, ROW."

Goldie

The day moved along slowly, like the boat. We didn't see the helicopter again. Towards late afternoon, we had not made as much progress as I had hoped. There definitely seemed to be a current in the water that was pulling us backwards, no matter how hard we tried to row. We were getting tired and were rowing very slowly. I knew we were going in the right direction, but it seemed to be taking a lot longer than I had thought.

"I'm sick of this boat, and so is Ginny," said Amanda.

"Okay, let's try another house," I said to myself as well as to the girls.

There was a house up ahead that looked promising, but when we got there all the windows were locked, so we had to row further along in the water to the next house. This one had an open upper window, which I thought somebody might have climbed out of in a rush. We paddled up to the window to look in.

"Well, it's okay, but not as nice as that other house," I said, standing up carefully and looking in. I tied the boat up to another pipe nearby then let it float out closer to the window.

"Maya, you hold the windowsill, and I'll climb in," I said.

Maya held the windowsill, Amanda held Maya's leg and Ginny, and I heaved myself up onto the windowsill and slid headfirst right into the room. It was a bedroom. This one was full of bookcases and books. It had twin beds and lots of toys!

"Boy, you should see this room. There are hundreds of books, probably with great pictures, just for us!" I yelled, my eyes catching familiar titles as I picked myself up from the strange spot I had landed in headfirst.

I turned towards the window and reached out a hand for Maya. Maya lunged into the room with me pulling her in, while the boat outside pushed away from the house, but was fastened on at the pipe.

"Hey, don't forget us!" yelled Amanda, alarmed. She gripped Ginny, and Amanda's eyes widened when she saw so much water between the house and the boat.

"Hang on, I'll be right there," I yelled towards the window.

I went to the closet and peered in. I looked around and up and saw an old wire hanger. I took it down and unwound it and straightened it out with a grunt and some groans. As I stuck it out the window, I leaned towards the boat, and hitched the hook part onto the rope, which it could just barely reach. I waited for a moment when the rope was slack, then pulled it towards me with the hanger. Then, grabbing the rope, I slowly hauled Amanda and Ginny and the boat in towards the house.

"Okay, Amanda: very slowly. Give me Ginny," I said.

"What about me?" asked Amanda.

"First Ginny, then you. It'll be okay, I promise," I reassured her.

Amanda held Ginny up as high as she could. Maya held onto my legs in the room and I leaned out and down as far as I could, and grabbed Ginny. I pulled Ginny and myself into the room, and Ginny leapt out of my arms before I could balance again. Ginny jumped onto one of the beds and licked herself. Then she jumped down and started to sniff and inspect every corner of the room.

"My turn!" yelled Amanda.

"Okay, take my hand and go slowly, Manda. I don't want you falling in again!" I said, sounding like my mother.

Very carefully, I offered Amanda both of my hands, and Amanda stood up while I pulled her inside the window. The boat pushed out from under Amanda's feet and for a moment she was dangling above the water as she was being pulled in. We pulled her up and into the window, and she and Maya and I all crashed on the floor together. Then we laughed and laughed. Amanda got up and went over to Ginny and picked her up. We all looked around.

"Do you think we should see if there is any food somewhere here like the other house?" asked Maya.

"Don't be silly. The food is in the kitchen and that's under water. Kitchens are supposed to be on the ground floor. I don't think anybody else would have thought about strangers like Mrs. Hendricks did, do you?" I asked.

"Nobody's like Mrs. Hendricks. I love her," said Amanda.

We all went over to the door and opened it. Then we went over to the bathroom door, which was open, and looked in, because we heard a little squeaking noise. Maya walked in first and said, "Oh, look! How cute, oh, cute, cute, cute! Amanda, look at this!"

The Mother Dog

We took quick, tiny steps until we were all the way in and looked into the bathtub. There were three golden-colored puppies fast asleep. A fourth was awake and having a drink from its mother. The mother, a Golden Retriever, looked concerned as she looked at our faces.

Ginny yelled, "Meow!" and jumped out of Amanda's arms, ran back into the bedroom and later we found her hiding under a bed. All the rest of the puppies woke up and started to crawl towards their mother's milk. Two of them started to fight over one nipple, pawing this way and that. Their eyes were open.

"Don't touch yet," I said. "The mother has to get to like us first, so just say nice things to her."

"Good dog, good dog," said Maya.

"I know, let's get some food for her. She looks very hungry," said Maya, running to the other room and getting some crackers. She brought them back into the bathroom and held one out to the mother dog.

"Here Goldie, good dog," said Maya, and let the mother dog sniff her hand and the cracker. The mother dog then leaned towards the cracker. Maya leaned towards the dog, too, and the dog opened her mouth and gently took the cracker. Maya smiled.

I petted the mother dog on the head, and she licked my hand. Maya very carefully petted one of the puppies that were busy sucking on its mother. The mother dog was very nice to Maya, but was watching her very closely.

Amanda wanted to pet one, too. She knelt down and stroked the little one by the mother dog's back leg.

"Look, this one is mine," she said.

"No way," I said. "You have that cat and that's too much anyway."

"Yeah, but it's really Maya's cat, so I get this puppy when the flood is over," replied Amanda.

"I bet Mom won't let you have one," I said.

"Yes, she will!" said Amanda with certainty.

Amanda put her hand on her favorite golden puppy, and gently pulled it away from its mother. The mother dog seemed to understand and leaned towards Amanda with a concerned look about her baby.

"It's okay, Goldie," said Amanda, petting the mother dog's forehead while she held the puppy. The mother dog seemed to understand Amanda, and lowered her head back down, yet kept her eyes on Amanda.

"Look, Amanda, we can only stay here one night, so stop falling in love with that puppy," I said. I was also totally in love with the puppy, but wouldn't tell Amanda just yet.

"I want to love my puppy. We could stay two nights, couldn't we?" she begged.

"No," I said. "We really have to keep going. But we can tell Mommy and Daddy about the puppy and come back and see if the people here will let us have it when it's a little older. For now, you can pet Ginny, okay?"

Amanda kissed her puppy and cuddled it and rocked it, and then I gently took it. Amanda stuck out her lower lip, while I put the puppy back with its mother. The puppy hunted for its mother's nipple and found it quickly, and it started sucking and pressing its tiny paws into its mother's stomach.

We hung out our clothes to dry, hoping they would be at least a little dryer by morning.

There was a damp and musty smell from the water below, which had soaked all the furniture downstairs. It was still light outside but we lit our candles. We all started yawning in chorus and giggled as we gazed into the caverns of each other's mouths.

"I'm hungry," said Amanda.

"You're always hungry," I answered, grabbing the peanut butter and fig bars.

"Here, now eat and go to sleep," I said.

"Let's read those books," suggested Amanda with her mouth full. "I want one with good pictures."

"There are some good ones," I said, pulling out some Dr. Seuss and Madeline books, and handing them to Amanda.

"Here are some fairy tales with pictures," said Maya, stacking some on top of the others.

"And I found *Charlotte's Web* which I always wanted to read again," I exclaimed. It looked so old that I imagined it could even belong to somebody who was grown up by now.

Amanda and I decided to sleep together in one bed, and Maya got into the other one with Ginny. The blankets were fluffy and the beds were heavenly for all of us.

Silence spread around the room like a sleepy mist comforting us, and the light began to fade. We looked at pictures, munched on more crackers, drank water or powdered milk and water, and petted Ginny.

Amanda jumped up and ran in to check the puppies, peered out the window on the way back, and asked, "Where is Mommy, Elizabeth?"

"We will find her tomorrow," I said, patting her shoulder, as she ran back to me and leapt on top of me.

"Move over," I added. "Read your books."

"I can't see now," she said, pulling the blankets over us.

"Try!"

"I'm trying," she said, yawning loudly, opening her eyes very widely.

My eyes fluttered as I tried to see the pages and keep the reality of our predicament away. In a while, I blew out the candles and slowly, one by one, we slid down under the covers and closed our eyes, dropping our books by our sides.

The evening turned into night and for us, the night went straight by, and none of us woke up. Even Ginny stayed asleep, I think. I had many dreams about boats and falling in the water, and yelling, "help," and sticky peanut butter in my mouth, until reality mixed with dreams and I didn't know which was which.

The Boat is Gone

The next morning, we got up and ran in to pet the puppies. Our hands got licked and licked clean by the mother dog, and we lovingly held each warm little puppy.

Ginny had slept with Maya, but crawled back under the bed after Maya got up. Ginny came out again when we got back into our bedroom to eat some more food. I wandered over to the window to look at the boat.

"Oh, no! The boat's gone!" I yelled.

Maya and Amanda came running over to the window, looked out, and Maya exclaimed, "Oh, no! Elizabeth, what are we going to do?"

"Well, let's go look out of all the windows and see if we can see it," I suggested. We ran to each window around the top floor of the house.

"No, not here," we said to each other as we checked each window. We ran into the next room.

"No, not here."

"No, not here."

"I want my mommy," said Amanda, not consoled by Ginny or the puppies or even her bear.

"Be quiet, Amanda, let me think," I said, feeling a little worried, and trying not to show it.

As I looked up, I barely saw something red peeking out from behind some tree branches. I suddenly felt sure it was the boat, and yelled, "There it is!" The girls looked to where I was pointing, and sure enough, we all saw it.

"How are we going to get it?" asked Maya.

"Let's swim over there," suggested Amanda.

"Don't be silly, Amanda, it's too cold and too far to swim, anyway," I said, but I was thinking the same thing.

I was a good swimmer, but the water was pretty cold. I looked at the two smaller girls in my charge. It had rained all night, the new day was cloudy and it looked like another storm would be coming soon. I didn't have a bathing suit. I didn't have a change of clothes. We needed that boat, or we would have to stay in this house until someone found us, and most of our food and water were still in the boat. Maybe we would end up on this rooftop.

We leaned on the windowsill, all in a row, staring at the boat, wishing we could reach out and pull it to us. Amanda looked at me.

"If I was bigger," Amanda said, "I would try to swim to the boat."

Maya looked at Amanda and then at me and then at the boat. Maya was a great swimmer, and I could see that she was thinking maybe she could swim to the boat. I looked at Amanda and then at Maya, and said, "No, you are not swimming to the boat, Maya!"

I looked at the boat, pointed my chin to my chest, stared out into space, and said, "*I am*, and you stay here." With that, I stripped off my large shirt, and just in my underpants, and without another look back, I jumped into the water.

The girls screamed, "Elizabeth, be careful!" I went under the water. It was over my head, but I bobbed up and waved, and yelled, "It's cold, here I go," and started to swim towards the boat.

The two girls watched me with wide eyes. Amanda told me later that I was getting smaller with each stroke. Maya told me she was thinking I was going to drown. Every time I lifted my arm out of the water, Maya later said her own arm was lifting and pretending she was swimming, too. She hardly realized she was doing it. It was a way she could try to help me.

I was halfway to the boat now and breathing hard. The water was very cold. I swam on my back for a while to regain my breath, then turned over and pushed on towards the boat, which I kept an eye on as much as I could. It was not too far away, and had stopped against a tree branch.

"You can do it, Elizabeth!" cried Maya. "You're almost there, just a little further!"

I was getting tired but knew I was closing in on our boat. I was swimming more slowly and getting colder, and I bumped into a plastic deck chair, which was floating by. I looked back at the girls and the house. They seemed so far away, but I kept on swimming.

The boat was getting bigger and bigger to my eyes, and suddenly there I was, grabbing up onto the sides. I was breathing very hard by now. As I lifted my head out of the water, I shook it to clear the water out of my ears, and then banged the side of it to get more water out. I wiped my bangs back across my forehead, and looked at the girls leaning out the window. They were yelling, "You did it! You did it!" and clapping their hands. I smiled in spite of the cold.

Resting for a minute, I then pulled myself around to the side of the boat near the back. It seemed to be the lowest place to try to get in. I heaved myself up onto the side, but fell back into the water. I tried again. I tried again and again, and could not get into the boat. I looked at the girls, who had stopped clapping and were now apparently holding their breath. I tried one more time. I just could not get into the boat. I was exhausted.

I looked over at the house, and at the window, and saw not just the two girls, but now I saw Goldie. I shivered and realized that I really could not get into the boat. I thought of pulling the boat back to the house, and so I went around to the bow, grabbed the rope, and started to pull the boat and swim. It was very difficult for me and I finally had to give up and go back to the side of the boat and hold on.

My teeth started to chatter. I was getting colder and more tired and wasn't making any progress. I thought maybe I should just try to swim back and leave the boat there, but I began to wonder if I had the strength left to swim back.

Suddenly I heard a huge splash, and saw Goldie in the water. It looked like she was swimming towards me. I wondered what she was doing, but I was glad for some kind of company anyway.

Soon I could hear Goldie breathing, and saw her eyes directly upon me. I could see a bit of the hair on Goldie's back, and her golden forehead and her black nose. Underneath the water I could

just make out Goldie's paws, pushing in their instinctive way, swimming as fast as any dog could possibly swim. Her nose was pointing right at me.

She swam right up to me and licked my face. I put my hand on her forehead to pet her, but Goldie swam to the rope right away and started to pull it. I swam over to the rope, too, and I started to pull it with her. Together we pulled and the boat started to move. Then it started to move a little more. We were swimming and pulling and breathing hard and blowing bubbles through the water that got into our mouths.

Amanda and Maya were yelling again. "You can do it, come on, here Goldie, here Goldie! Come on, Elizabeth!"

I was extremely tired and cold, but Goldie was encouraging me on and so I kept warmer by just swimming and pulling as hard as I could. It was easier when I pulled at the same time as Goldie.

Branches of trees got in the way of the boat, and other objects floating by. I had to go around the back of the boat and push the boat away to get it untangled from the branches. I swam back to the rope and Goldie and I swam on. It seemed to be taking forever!

Maya and Amanda were hanging out of the window yelling. I felt like I couldn't lift my arms one more time. I looked up at the girls a few times as I swam.

Finally we swam up to the house and I tied the rope onto the pipe, making sure the knot would hold this time. I pulled the boat over to the window and held one arm up to Maya.

The mother dog swam next to me and I held onto the windowsill with one hand. Then Maya and Amanda grabbed my other arm and pulled together, and I heaved myself up to the window.

"Okay, pull, pull, pull," I commanded, and the girls pulled like they were saving my life, and finally I was over the windowsill and sliding right onto the floor past the girls. Everyone was breathing hard. I sat there on the floor in a puddle of water, and the girls kneeled down and gave me a big hug.

Maya said, "You're so cold, Elizabeth. Get into bed, quick." But I said, "What about Goldie?" We looked at each other in alarm and stood up and leaned out the window. She was gone.

"Oh, no!" I yelled through my chattering teeth.

Covered in goose bumps, and generally frozen all over, I grabbed a blanket from the bed and threw it around my shoulders and ran back to the window. We stretched our necks out to see where the dog had gone. We looked down into the murky water. She was nowhere to be seen. Amanda started to cry. Maya started to cry. I started to cry. We looked at each other crying. We hugged. I shivered.

Then we all knew what each one was thinking, and without a word, we all ran into the bathroom to cry with the puppies.

We stopped in our tracks when we saw her. There was Goldie, already in the bathtub, very wet, and feeding her babies.

"How did you get there?" we asked Goldie, hugging her and petting her. "Good dog, good dog!" we all told her.

I followed the trail of water that Goldie had made, and saw that it came from the stairs.

"Hey, I know how she did it. She probably went under the water and found an open door or window, and swam underwater over to the stairs and got in that way. Goldie's a smart dog!" I said, coming back to pet Goldie on the head. Goldie was so wet. Even though I was shivering and cold, I grabbed a towel and rubbed her back and head, and peered at her eyes and said, "Thank you, Goldie!"

The Cow

With our boat back by the window, we loaded it up with all our damp clothes, and put on the large, grown-up shirts we had found in the bedroom of the previous house.

We petted the puppies one last time. Amanda left a box of crackers for Goldie, and four crackers with peanut butter on them in case she wanted them. Then we climbed slowly and carefully, one by one, back into our boat. We were getting to be quite good at not even rocking the boat too much. We all sat down in our places.

"All right," I said to Maya, "let's row: One, two, three, ROW, one, two, three, ROW! One, two, three, ROW!" we chanted.

Amanda was looking at us rowing, and petting Ginny, and then she yelled, "Goodbye, Goldie, we'll come back soon. We love you!"

"One, two, three, ROW, one, two, three, ROW," we chanted, and this time, Amanda joined in the chanting.

We rowed and rowed for hours. We sang songs from nursery school to keep up the rhythm. "The wheels on the bus go round and round," we sang and hummed.

We rowed past more trees, several more houses, lots of floating furniture, mattresses, baby bottles, plastic bags, pieces of wood, garbage, newspapers, many ducks and a few birds. The sun was shining in between the clouds and despite all our troubles we were just about warm enough to be happy.

"Look! There's a dead cow!" screamed Maya, pointing at an upside-down, very dead, cow.

"Oh, yuck! Keep on rowing," I said in disgust, but I could hardly stop looking at the poor, drowned creature.

"Let's stop and touch it," said Amanda.

"Don't be ridiculous, it's probably got flies and maggots by now," suggested Maya.

"Yeah," I said, steering the boat over to the cow.

Maya reached out and tried to touch it. She screamed.

"Yuck!" she said.

"I want to touch it," whined Amanda again.

"Go ahead," I dared her.

Amanda reached over the side of the boat as I paddled by the huge dead body, and touched its leg.

"Yuck, it's all muddy and stiff and cold," she said, pulling her finger to her side and wiping it about a hundred times.

"Okay, say goodbye. We have to move on," I said, feeling kind of sad for the horrible death that cow must have suffered, trying to swim, maybe trying to get to her calf somewhere. I looked around and didn't see anything like a calf. That would have been too horrible, I thought, and started rowing furiously.

In a while, we all heard an engine sound in the distance.

"Look, look! Is that another helicopter?" said Maya. "I think it is! Let's wave. Come on!"

"Hey, helllllloooooo! Here we are!" we all yelled as the helicopter flew nearer and nearer.

"Don't fly past us this time, we're here!" I said, picking up my dirty white shirt and waving it so the pilot could see us. We were so busy looking up that we didn't see the tree. Crash! Bang! The boat started rocking horribly.

"Whoa!" I yelled, dropping my shirt and grabbing the sides of the boat. The cat jumped out of Amanda's arms and into the water.

"Oh, no! Ginny's in the water," cried Maya. Amanda reached out towards Ginny who was really a good swimmer by instinct, even though she hated the water. Ginny was trying to swim back to the boat.

"Meow! Meow!" she cried.

Amanda reached and reached, saying, "Come on, kitty, kitty, kitty, come on, you can do it!" I grabbed an oar and started turning the boat a little so we were closer to Ginny. But Ginny seemed to be floating away from the boat, no matter how hard she paddled her little paws. Then I started rowing the boat in her direction. Amanda reached as far as she could and almost touched her, but one oar slipped from my hand and I dropped it into the boat, the boat turned to the side and Ginny was even further away. I grabbed the oar again and pulled hard so the boat turned around and aimed back towards our swimming cat.

"Meow!" yelled Ginny, as she kept paddling with her paws.

"We're coming, we're coming," I said loudly.

"Come on, Ginny!" coached Amanda.

The boat was getting closer to Ginny, and I was paddling nearer and nearer. Maya leaned down again and reached as far as she could. Amanda held onto her legs so she wouldn't fall in, and finally Maya could just about touch poor, wet Ginny. She then lunged at Ginny's collar and pulled her up and into the boat.

THE FLOOD

Ginny was so very, very wet. Her hair was flat on her body and she looked as skinny as a cat who hadn't eaten for a week. Her whiskers were drooping. She looked very sad and miserable.

"Meow!" she said. "Meow!"

"Meow," said Maya back to her.

Amanda wrapped her up with my shirt and then put her under her coat so she wouldn't get too cold, and tried to rub her dry.

"That's okay, Ginny, you're going to be all right," said Amanda. "What a good swimmer you are!" she added.

"Meow," came a muffled sound from under Amanda's coat.

I searched the sky, listening like a deer, but I couldn't hear an engine, and I couldn't see that helicopter through the low clouds.

The Sail

The helicopter had flown right past us and into the distance, the pilot probably never even spotting our boat or hearing our screams.

I picked up the oars, wiped my hair from my forehead, and handed one oar to Maya.

"Okay, let's row again. They probably didn't see us because we were under the tree. Maybe they will turn around and see us if they come back this way," I said. "But maybe they won't, so let's just keep going."

"One, two, three, ROW," said Amanda. We all chimed in together, and off we went.

A cold wind had come up and was blowing onto our red cheeks as we paddled the boat along. The harder we rowed, the more the wind seemed to push us backwards.

I looked at the water with its strange items floating by from all the people's houses that were flooded. I saw a blue jacket, and a red ball and big plastic water bottles. I saw a purple, soggy pillow, and a broom stuck in some branches. A broom!

Imagine that. I thought about sweeping the kitchen, which I always had to do at home.

We rowed and rowed. It was slow. I wished we could go faster. If we had an engine, we could get to the Community Center really quickly, I thought. My back was starting to hurt, and a blister was bothering me on my palm. I wished that maybe I could make a sail with that tarp I had my feet on top of. But we didn't have a mast. We rowed a little more.

"The broom!" I said aloud.

"What?" asked Maya.

"The broom," I said again.

"I know. What about the broom?" asked Maya looking at me half bored.

"Turn around, we are turning around, now!" I commanded, as I pushed my oar backwards.

"Why?" asked Amanda.

"Because I found a mast," I replied, loudly. "Well, sort of a mast. It'll do," I mumbled.

I worked my oar and we started to turn back towards the broom that was stuck in the branch of a tree, and we kept rowing until we were right alongside of it. I leaned over and grabbed the handle with one hand, and with a tug, I tried to get it out from the branches. It was stuck. I wiggled and yanked it, and pushed it and pulled it. The boat began to rock.

"Hey!" yelled Amanda. "No rocking the boat."

"Be quiet, I can't help it. Just hold tight and hold Ginny," I commanded, like the captain of a ship.

I finally dislodged the broom with a huge tug, grabbed it with both hands, and pulled it into the boat.

"Look! We have a pole for the sail," I said with a satisfied smile all over my face.

I turned around and leaned towards the bow. Then I pulled the rope from the front of the boat towards me, removed it from the bow and pulled it to where I was sitting. I wrapped the tarp around the broomstick at the top and at the bottom of the pole, tying the tarp once on the top and once down the middle. It slid off. I tried again, this time pulling it much tighter. This time the tarp stayed on. The girls held the edges of the tarp and held up the broom for me while I invented the new sail. The only trouble was that there was no place to anchor the rope down onto the boat.

"We need something to hold this down," I said.

We looked around for something in the water. There were so many strange things floating by, but nothing seemed to answer our need. I scratched my head, scanning the garbage, and probably looked disappointed to Maya.

"What about me?" asked Maya.

"Hey! What about you. Great idea," I said.

So Maya crouched down and held up the pole, trying to wedge it against the seat. As soon as she did, the wind gently started to fill up the blue tarp and when I rowed, too, the boat started to move—slowly at first, then a little faster.

Amanda took Maya's oar and copied my rowing. Ginny sat on the bow of the boat, leading the way. Maya knelt with her legs wrapped around the bristles of the broom to keep herself and the broom steady. She had to lean back when the wind became stronger and the sail really started to work.

But then the wind gusted up suddenly and Maya lost her hold on the sail and the mast and the boat rocked as she tried to grab the mast. I reached for the sail as it started to fall over. I grabbed it just before it hit the water then pulled it, hand over hand, into the boat. My oar flipped out of the oarlock and into the water and started to float away. Amanda put her oar down into the boat and leaned forward and grabbed Ginny's collar with one hand, and Maya's leg to keep her from falling out of the boat, with the other.

Maya grabbed the floating oar while still holding onto the broomstick. Then Amanda let go of Maya's leg, and grabbed onto my oar, as it floated back towards her. She pulled the broomstick up again with her other hand. Grunting and moaning, I circled my fingers around the tarp-sail with my other hand. Maya grabbed part of the sail to steady it.

We all sighed, and, again, with a little help from my oars, the boat started moving again. Pretty soon we were moving much more quickly than we had been just rowing. Only we were moving in the wrong direction!

"I know I can do this," I said, trying to remember how we had sailed in another boat once at the lake. I dipped my oar in straight down, and held it hard against the pull of the water, turning the boat. The sail crinkled and then ballooned a little bit the other way, and by some sort of magic, we were now sailing in the right direction with me holding the full sail stretched out with one hand, and trying to row with the other. Amanda was trying to steer and row with my oar and Maya was holding up the pole and guiding the sail.

"We're sailing a little bit! The wind is great for this! Aren't we clever!" I said, shivering. The other two nodded, half smiling and half serious with the business at hand. We sailed along like this for a short while. It was fun in a strenuous sort of way.

"I'm getting tired of this," said Maya. "And anyway, I don't think it works that much," she added.

I said, "Hold it a little bit longer. I think we're getting nearer to the Community Center! Hey! I can see the top of the Community Center!"

"It looks crooked," I said after a moment. "Hey … something's different! It looks funny. You guys! Where is the hill behind it?"

"What do you mean?" asked Maya.

"I mean, there used to be a hill behind it. I can't see one now, can you?" I answered.

"No, I can't see a hill," said Maya.

"I can't see a hill, either," said Amanda.

Maya dropped the sail into the boat and paddled towards the Community Center.

"I can see the bottom! It's getting shallower. Look! I can see stuff on the bottom. I think I see a toaster," said Amanda, peering over the side into the water next to the boat.

"Keep rowing, Mandy. We're going to be there really soon," said Maya stashing the broom and the tarp down onto the floor of the boat.

We were only about a hundred feet from the land, the first dry land we had seen since leaving our house. As we neared the land, Maya grabbed the oar from Amanda, who didn't mind a bit, and they switched places.

Amanda, now at the back of the boat again, pulled Ginny towards her gently with both hands and held her close to her body. Maya and I rowed nearer and nearer to the edge of the bank. Finally, we got so close to the water's edge, that I jumped out and splashed into the water up to my knees, and pulled the rocking boat nearer to the shore. Maya jumped out into the water and helped pull the boat up to dry land. The boat finally stalled as it touched the muddy bottom.

Ginny jumped out of Amanda's arms, right into
the mud. She shook her paws in disgust, ran to a
tree and climbed up to the first branch. She sat
down and started to lick her muddy paws.

"Ginny, come here! Come down, right now!"
yelled Amanda, scrambling out of the boat,
running over to the tree. She looked up at Ginny
and put her hands on her hips, with a combination
of authority and resignation.

She turned around to face us, knowing somehow
that Ginny was going to stay there anyway, and
looked at Maya and me, slipping and sliding on
the steep, grassy bank, still trying to pull the

boat all the way out of the water. She came back over and grabbed the side of the boat and heaved it along with us until the boat was right up on the muddy bank and could not float away.

"We did it! We did it!" we shouted to each other, hugging as we deliberately slid our shoes back and forth in the mud.

The Discovery

"Let's explore," I said, looking towards the crumbling Community Center all covered in mud from the hill slide.

"Yeah, let's find out what's going on there," said Maya.

"Yeah, I'm coming, too. What about Ginny?" asked Amanda, grabbing our teddy bears.

"She will probably follow us, don't worry," I answered.

"I'm getting into drier clothes," said Maya.

"Me, too," said Amanda.

"Me too," I said.

We took off our muddy shoes, one by one, and pulled on our jeans, still a bit wet, and exchanged our huge grown-up shirts that had been our only dry clothing under our coats, for our own.

"Hold onto my shoulder and don't put your sock into the mud!" I told Amanda.

"Okay," she said. She put her sock right into the mud.

"Yuck," she moaned.

"I told you, now hold onto me and go slowly."

"That's better, Amanda. Now let me hold onto your shoulder," I added, slipping my muddy shoes off and putting on my jeans, while holding onto Amanda. Maya held her other shoulder while continuing to change clothes.

"I'm sure glad you like me better as a pole than a sister!" said Amanda.

"Yeah, I do," I grinned.

Then we put our coats back on, and I stuffed the bears into my pockets, and we were ready to go.

We slid along the muddy bank as if we had skis on, and worked our way towards the Community Center. As we pushed and pushed along, mud was clogging the soles of our shoes. Ginny was straggling behind us, catching up. It seemed like we were moving in slow motion.

When we got to the Community Center, we discovered a horrible mess of mud, and cars that had turned over, and the whole half of the building that was all smashed in. The mountainside had slid right on top of our Community Center: I think my cold, rosy cheeks turned pale.

"That's our car. That one over there," I said, pointing to one of the ones that was turned over. "Oh, my God! Where's Mom, where's Dad?" I said sloshing towards the car, and looking inside.

"It's empty," I said, even though I knew it had to be.

We looked around. The whole deserted place was a huge catastrophe. There were yellow ribbons saying "Caution, Keep Out!" around parts of the building. There were muddy tire tracks, quite big. We looked at each other with our mouths and eyes wide open.

Then, from a distance, we could hear the sound of the helicopter again, and it was getting louder. We all squinted our eyes and saw a tiny dot in the sky. Then it got bigger. Pretty soon, it was no longer a dot. It was the helicopter. Hoping to get help, we dropped our investigation of the building, and tried to get the helicopter's attention. It was flying lower. I walked as quickly as I could back to the boat, trying not to slip and fall down. My feet were caked with mud. I grabbed the sail and plodded back to the girls, with my feet even heavier and bigger with mud, and threw the tarp to the girls.

"Quick, spread this out and wave it. Quick, before they go by again!" I yelled.

Ginny ran away from the flapping tarp. Amanda picked up a side near me and Maya grabbed the other side, and we flapped it and waved it and shouted to the sky.

"Here we are, here we are!" we all yelled as loudly as we possibly could.

Then we saw somebody leaning out of the helicopter door. But the helicopter just flew on by: we all groaned in unison.

"They didn't see us! How could they not see us?" I yelled in utter frustration.

Just then, the helicopter turned around and flew back in our direction.

"Yell, they're coming back, yell! Hey, Hey, here we are! Here we are!" we yelled and yelled, shaking the blue tarp again.

Then we saw a hand waving at us from the helicopter.

"They've seen us! They've seen us! Yeah! Helloooooo!" we all cried.

The noise of the helicopter was deafening. It came right over us and high above us there was a man being lowered down towards us. When he got quite near, through the noise of the wind and the engine, it seemed he was yelling, "Hello! Are you Elizabeth and Amanda and Maya?"

We all screamed at him. "Yes, we are!"

"We've been looking all over for you," he shouted back.

The man in a blue uniform was being lowered right down almost on top of our heads. The wind

THE FLOOD

from the propellers was blowing everything on the ground around, and our clothes and hair were blowing as if we were in a hurricane.

"We're looking for our moms and dads. We think they were in this mudslide," I yelled.

"We know! You can hitch a ride with us for a few miles," yelled the man back to us.

"Who wants to be the first one to go up?" he asked, dangling from a rope as he got nearer to us.

"I do!" said Amanda, bravely.

The man was sitting in a safety harness with wide shoulder straps. He clamped something like a safety harness around Amanda's stomach and upper legs, and up she went with the man holding tightly onto her. The wind from the twirling wings seeming to push them down hard as they went up and up to the helicopter door, and into the helicopter.

Over the noise of the helicopter we could faintly hear Amanda screaming.

"You're all right," I yelled, amazed at the whole procedure.

"Who's next," yelled the man as loud as he could when he came down again.

"Me!" yelled Maya back to him, her hair blowing in every direction.

He put her into the safety harness and up they went. He held onto her as she screamed, too.

Then he came down and said to me, "Are you ready?" I could just hear the girls yelling "Ginny, Ginny, Ginny."

"No. We can't go without our cat," I yelled back.

I pointed to the cat standing nearby. Her fur was blowing and her eyes were almost completely closed. She obviously didn't like the noise or the strong wind, but clearly she had no intention of being left behind, even if she had to go up in a helicopter!

I went over, bent down and tried to grab Ginny. Ginny started to run away. I took off after her, clumping along with my muddy shoes. Ginny ran quite far until the wind from the helicopter was not blowing so hard on her, and the sound wasn't blasting her ears. Then she stopped and looked up at me.

"Meow," she said.

"I know you're scared, but you will be okay," I answered Ginny. I walked slowly towards her and bent down with my hand stretched out.

"Meow," said Ginny again.

I moved closer and slowly picked her up, brushed some mud off her feet, and put her whole body inside my coat, enclosing her from the wind and noise. I walked back, leaning against the wind, towards the helicopter where the man stood.

The man reached out his hand, took Ginny, and put her into a huge pocket in his coat and zipped it up so just Ginny's head was outside. Ginny yelled, "Meow! Meow!"

He showed me how to get into the safety harness, and as we swung up into the air, I yelled out all the sadness and fear I had held inside.

"Help! Whoa! Help! Yippee!" I screamed to the sky.

We were pulled up through an enormous blast of thundering wind to the door of the helicopter. I got into the helicopter first, with the help of another man in the helicopter, and then the man on the rope got in, with Ginny's head still poking out of his coat. Two great girls smiled at me and my eyes grew as large as an owl's, and they circled their arms around my shoulders.

"Meow, meow," said Ginny as the helicopter lifted up higher into the sky.

From the helicopter we could now see that the huge mudslide had really crushed a lot of our Community Center.

"Wow," I said. "What a mess. Do you know what happened to the people who were in the mudslide?" I asked, fearing what I might hear.

"Well, you girls are quite famous now, you know. Everybody has been looking for you and has been very worried about you. So we know who your parents are, and I can tell you that they were injured, but they'll be all right. I am going to have to put you back down onto the ground soon in a safer place where cars can drive, and a nice woman in an ambulance will take you to the hospitals to see your parents. You all look fine. Nobody hurt?" said the man.

We looked at each other in a special way, in relief, because it was the first time we knew where our parents were or that they weren't buried alive.

"No, we're fine. We just want to see our parents," said Maya.

"We looked for you but couldn't see you. What a relief to spot you today!" said the pilot.

The helicopter came down towards the earth, or actually, it felt like the earth came up towards us! It landed with a few gentle bumps, and the nice men helped us out of it. The wind was ferocious and the noise hurt our ears.

When all three of us were on the ground, the pilot said goodbye through a loudspeaker, and we jumped into each other's arms hearing the surprisingly loud voice.

"Goodbye!" we all yelled. "Thank you!"

The man in the blue uniform got back into the helicopter and they lifted off, blowing us almost right off our feet.

THE FLOOD

"Goodbye!" we yelled again at the same time, holding tightly onto each other and Ginny, and looking up, as it got quieter and quieter, and smaller and smaller in the sky.

The Ambulance

The ground was dry in the place we were standing. Trees were clear of the water and appeared to be their normal height, and there was a house with a front door you didn't have to swim in through.

Then we saw the ambulance. It was racing along towards us and pulled up near us with a screech and stopped. A woman in another kind of blue uniform opened the ambulance door and jumped out.

"Oh, my goodness, there you are! They radioed me that you would be here. My name is Brenda. Are you okay?" she asked, putting her arms around Amanda and Maya, and looking at me with a little frown.

"Oh, yes. We're okay, but we want to see our parents. We want to see our moms and dads," I said, my throat suddenly tight.

"Of course, you do. And you shall see them today! Are you hungry?"

"No, but just tired of peanut butter," said Amanda.

"When can we see them?" Maya yelled.

"You don't have to yell now. You can see them as soon as we can drive to them," said the woman.

"I miss my mommy," said Amanda.

"Me, too," said Maya.

"Me, too," I said.

We all walked over to the ambulance, but before we got in, we scraped the mud off our shoes the best we could by using sticks we found, and then we looked up at the huge red and white ambulance.

"Have you ever been in an ambulance?" the woman asked us.

"No, but it looks like fun!" I said, eyeing it with the flashing lights at the top. I scraped some more mud off the soles of my shoes.

"I'm afraid that is all we have right now, although you three girls do look just fine to me. Are you sure you don't have any cuts or bruises?"

"I do," said Amanda, holding out her hand, her lower lip jutting out. The woman looked very hard at Amanda's hand and I am sure she could not see anything, but she kissed it better anyway, and Amanda smiled and said, "All better."

"Okay, then, let's get into this ambulance and I'll take you to the hospitals," said the woman.

"Oh, we're fine," I said, "we don't need a hospital, we just need our mommies."

"No, we're going to the hospital to see your mommy," said the woman, smiling.

"Oh," I said. "Oh, yeah. What's the matter with our mommy? What happened to her? Is she okay?" I asked. I am sure she saw my face drop and my body stop breathing, as still as a listening statue.

"She's fine now," said the woman. "She was in the mudslide and has a few cuts and bruises. She also sleeps a lot, trying to remember what happened. She got a little bump on her head."

Amanda started to cry. Then she looked up to the woman in the blue uniform and said, "I will kiss it better."

"Where's my mommy? Does she have a bump on her head?" asked Maya.

"I met your mother. She is okay, and she's in the hospital where Amanda's and Elizabeth's father is, so we'll visit her there, too, when we visit your father," said the woman to Maya who was looking worried, expecting the worst. "Your father is in the same hospital as Elizabeth's father." Maya smiled in relief, and said, "Well, let's go!"

"Why are they in two different hospitals?" I asked.

"Well, there were so many people injured in the mudslide, that we needed to take them to whatever hospital had beds free," answered Brenda.

"Oh," I said, wondering about all those people.

"The cat will have to stay here," said Brenda.

"No! Ginny has to come with us! She was with us all the way!"

"I am afraid cats are not allowed in ambulances," said Brenda.

"Then I'm not going," said Amanda.

"Me neither," said Maya.

"Me neither," I said.

Brenda put her hands on her hips, and didn't say a word. She just stood there, eyeing us. Then she said, "Okay, just this once."

"Yes!" I said.

"Yes!" said Maya and Amanda together.

So I got to put Ginny into the back of the ambulance.

"Meow! Meow!" said Ginny, who did not seem to like cars or helicopters or ambulances at all. She crawled in between something like a bed and a wall, and curled up and hid.

Then we all climbed into the ambulance. I got in the front and fastened my seatbelt. The woman helped Amanda and Maya sit in the back seats, and fastened a safety belt around each of them.

"Okay, here we go," she said as she climbed into the driver's seat and fastened her own safety belt.

We drove near enough to the landslide area that I could see our upturned car again, but I decided not to mention it. I looked ahead at the road and smiled to myself, knowing that at last we would be with our parents.

The Ride to the City

The ambulance, with the three of us looking out of the windows, moved off towards the city. It was thrilling as we finally sped towards our mothers and fathers.

I kind of missed our adventures with the boat, but I knew I was really ready to be a little girl again and let somebody else take charge of things and tell me what to do, until I got a bit older.

Amanda was holding both teddy bears and Maya had her arm around Amanda.

Sitting in front, I was watching us moving quickly through the countryside towards the city. I missed my mom very much and had been really quite brave up to now, but suddenly I felt like crying, even though I knew it was all going to be okay now. I peeked around to see if anybody was looking at me, and I wiped a tear from my cheek. I looked over at Brenda who was driving so quickly. Then I wondered, as I wiped another tear away, if I might like to be an ambulance driver when I grew up.

"When will we be there?" asked Amanda.

"In about half an hour more," said Brenda. Amanda wiggled in her seat behind her safety belt. I know she felt like jumping up and down with excitement, but she had to wait until we stopped. I could see she didn't really want to wait, though.

The countryside rushed by, the trees, the cows, some horses, some cars and trucks, a gas station, some small stores, then some bigger stores, and more traffic, and soon houses all along the road, and then traffic lights. We were back in the big city. It seemed noisy and busy and everybody seemed to be moving along so quickly.

"We are almost there—it's about another mile," said Brenda.

We looked out of the window, to the left and to the right and straight ahead. The ambulance turned a corner, and then another corner, and then sped on towards a large, square building. This building was the largest we saw on the whole trip.

"There it is!" I said. "I bet that's it!"

"You're right," said Brenda. "Here we are, and we can go right into the hospital through that driveway." And so we did—right up to the hospital entrance. We drove past the front, and came to a halt outside the Emergency Entrance, and someone opened the back of the ambulance almost before we stopped. Ginny kept hiding. Everyone had forgotten about her just then.

"Come with us," said another woman, after opening the ambulance door. So we took off our seat belts. Maya helped Amanda.

Then we jumped out of the ambulance with Brenda's help. I took Amanda's hand, and one of the women took Amanda's other hand, and Maya took Brenda's hand, and we began a long walk down a corridor to an elevator. Ginny stayed in the ambulance, hiding.

We got into the elevator and looked at each other. I was still holding Amanda's other hand. Maya stood alone, and put her hands behind her back. She stared at the buttons.

"Fifth floor," said Brenda to Maya, and Maya quickly found the button and pressed it for the fifth floor.

When we got to the fifth floor, we all stepped out and followed the woman down the long corridor to a room. The sign on the door said "Shirley Selby." The woman knocked lightly and waited. A faint voice from inside said, "Come in."

I opened the door and pulled Amanda behind me as I walked in. Maya and Brenda followed us in.

The room was bright, impressive in its whiteness and cleanliness–which was an extreme contrast with us!

"Mommy!" Amanda and I cried out at the same time, and we ran over to her and gently hugged and kissed her bandaged head.

"Slow down," said Brenda, who stood just inside the door. "Your mom has a head wound. She needs to be quiet."

Our mother looked at both of us. She had a questioning look in her eyes. Her head was bandaged and her arms were, too. Then her memory was apparently jolted. She stared at us and slowly I could see she was starting to remember.

Although she was still a little dazed, her memory was clearly returning, like a dimmer light being switched on. Her eyes darted quickly, back and forth from Maya to Amanda to me. Tiny drops of perspiration glistened on her forehead. She glanced at the lights and closed her eyes for a second and then looked again. It seemed to me that a million confusing memories were flooding through her mind. She smiled and raised her eyebrows, and scrunched up her eyes. She breathed in a deep breath and I could see, she finally knew that we were her children, safe and sound, and that she was our mother.

She stretched out her arms and put them around each one of us. I felt her warm cheek and her breath. She closed her eyes, and said, "My children, my children," and tears rolled down her cheeks and touched mine.

Maya was just behind Amanda and me. I knew she was watching and wishing to be hugged, too. I saw her look at this scene of love, and look down. She brushed her shoe back and forth.

"Maya, hello. Have you been with my girls?" Mom asked her, holding out her hand towards Maya, and looking at her right in the eyes.

"Yes, I have. We sure wondered where you were!" she said, breathlessly, walking close enough to let Mom hold her, too.

We all cried in happiness, our bodies wet and shaking, and holding on tightly to each other.

"Mommy, why didn't you come home?" asked Amanda. "We waited and waited for you and then we had to leave the house in our boat to find you."

"Oh, my dear, dear ones. I would have found you if I could have, but I don't know, I can't remember. Oh, yes, now I remember! I was in some kind of accident. I just don't remember anything. My dear girls! What has happened? How long have I been here? How long has it been since we didn't come home?" she asked us, looking at us with love and concern.

"Can't you remember, Mommy?" asked Amanda.

Mom shook her head, trying to remember.

"Four days, I think, but it feels like a year," I said. "And two nights that we spent in other people's houses."

"What houses?" asked mom, her forehead developing a crease.

"Some houses that nobody lived in because of the flood," I answered reassuringly.

"We found some puppies and I want one," added Amanda.

"Well, Mandy, my dear sweet one. Puppies. Well, well, maybe. What kind of puppies? I don't know. We'll have to ask your father. Oh, my goodness, where is your father?" asked Mom, remembering Daddy after four days of sleeping.

"We think he's okay, but he's in another hospital," I answered.

"A hospital?" exclaimed Mom. "Is he all right? What happened to him? Let's go and see him right now!" Mom started to push the sheet away and get out of bed.

Amanda and Maya looked at me with bulging eyes, and I put out my hand for Mom as she tried to get up. We thought it was a great idea. Mom stood up slowly and put her hand to her head. Then she felt the bandage and said, "Just a minute. Where's a mirror?"

"There, Mom," I said, spotting a round one with a wooden handle on a white table in the corner.

Mom walked gingerly over to the corner with me, followed closely by us girls. She picked up the mirror and looked into it. Maya was standing close behind her. Amanda was holding onto my shirt.

"Oh, heavens! Look at me! Maybe I should lie down for a minute," she said, putting the mirror down, and resting her arms around Maya's and my shoulders and walking with us back to the bed.

I could see Mom turning a little pale as she sank back into her hospital bed with a new understanding smile for us.

"Hmm. I think I'd better stay here for a while longer. I guess I haven't stood up much for the past few days that I can remember. I think I really have to rest for a bit longer. Okay?" she said to us, as Maya and I looked into her eyes and I studied her nose and mouth and the wisps of hair sticking out from the bandage around her face.

"Mommy, you really should rest," I said, becoming a parent to my own mom. "I think we'll go and find Daddy ourselves, and we'll come back later to see how you are doing? Okay?"

My mother smiled in gratitude, probably relieved to have her memory back and happy to have us back, but also clearly feeling very ready for a little more sleep. As soon as the water from the flood subsided and she felt better, I knew she would gather us together with Dad, and go back home.

The nurse reached her warm hands out and took Amanda's and my hands. Maya took my other hand.

"Bye, Mom. We'll see you later and tell you how Dad is doing, okay?" I said, as I saw my mother's eyes getting tired. I leaned over and kissed her on the cheek. Amanda hugged her and kissed her on the cheek after I did. Our mom kissed us each on the forehead, and put her hand on our cheeks.

"Bye, my sweeties, I love you. Come back later and we shall have a lovely time together," she said, and closed her eyes to continue a lovely deep, healing sleep. As we craned our heads for one last glimpse, Brenda led us out of the room and back down to the waiting ambulance.

Daddy

"Shall we go to the other hospital to see your fathers?" asked Brenda with a twinkle in her eye, letting Amanda press the elevator button.

"Yes, yes, yes! And can we have the siren on?" I asked, jumping up and down with Maya and Amanda.

"Well, I am sorry, but we can't. We will just be like the rest of the cars and drive just fast enough to get there quickly and still be safe, okay?" she said.

"Oh, heck. But it will be fun anyway, huh, Amanda?" I put my arm around Amanda. Amanda looked up to me with a toothy smile.

"We saw Mommy!" I said to her. "Pretty soon we can go home, okay?" I added.

"I hope so," answered Amanda, looking back at Brenda.

"We have to see when the flood waters subside," answered Brenda.

"I want to see my mommy," said Maya.

"You can see her very soon, Maya," said Brenda.

A large, sweet smile spread over Maya's dirty face.

"Let's get out of here!" she said, as the elevator door opened.

We passed the Emergency Room and walked through a corridor back to our same ambulance.

"This is so great," I said. "I can't wait to tell my friends."

"You can tell them about your boating adventures, too," said Brenda as she climbed in. We got back into our old seats and Brenda started the engine.

"They won't believe me, I bet," I said, starting to imagine myself telling my friend Kirsten what had happened. "They won't believe the part about all the food Mrs. Hendricks left for us."

"She didn't leave it for us, silly," said Maya.

"Yes, she did. She knew we were coming, somehow."

"Yeah, but not us, she just thought somebody might turn up," said Maya, twisting her head around to look for Ginny.

"Well, anyway, not many people would have left out food for some dumb stranger, right?" I asserted.

"Oh, I don't know. I would have. Some people are nice. They think about ways to help birds and dogs and other people, too," said Maya, turning her head the other way.

"And goldfish, and snakes, and chickens, and birds, and squirrels, and horses, and cows," added Amanda.

I stretched my hand over onto Amanda's knee and said, "And ants, Amanda."

"Meow," said a little voice from the floor of the ambulance.

"And cats!" said Amanda, leaning down to pet Ginny. Ginny purred. Maya breathed a sigh of relief, hearing that Ginny was safe.

We put our safety belts on and drove out of the driveway into the street, and were again on our way. Amanda pulled the bears from my coat pockets.

"Everything is okay now," she whispered into their ears.

After driving about half an hour, just as we were arriving at the other hospital, Maya said to Brenda, "I want to see my mommy right away—you got to see your mommy already—so I want to see my mommy first. And I want them to come with me. You can see your dad right after I see my mom, okay?" She looked at Brenda, and then at us.

"I want to see my daddy now," said Amanda, petting her bear.

"Me, too," I said. "But we *did* see our mommy first, and I think we could wait a little bit to see Daddy. I want to see Maya's mommy, too, don't you?" I said to Amanda with a cheerful, encouraging face.

"Yeah, but we can see Daddy first, can't we?" she whined, now clutching her bear.

"We could, but that wouldn't be fair to Maya, would it?" I answered.

"No," said Amanda, looking scrunched up and not very convinced. "Okay, but we can't stay long," she said to Maya.

"Thanks, Amanda. Thanks, Elizabeth," said Maya, stretching her neck a bit to see the second huge hospital just coming into view. Ginny poked her nose out for another pet from Amanda, and then crawled back into her little safe place and probably went to sleep.

The ambulance came to a stop at the Emergency Entrance, and we climbed out and followed Brenda to the elevator. Amanda got to press the button, floor five again. We left our tummies on the ground floor as the elevator went swiftly up to the fifth floor without a stop.

The doors opened and we walked down the corridor straight to a door labeled, "Yoko Hanako." Maya walked in first. Her mother was sitting up in bed reading a book, with her leg in a cast propped up in the air.

"Mommy! Mommy!" cried Maya running over to hug her.

"Maya-chan, where have you been?" she said as she hugged Maya." I have been so worried about you! Look at your dirty face? Oh, hello, Elizabeth, hello, Amanda! This is quite a party! Tell me where you have been. We were worried sick!" she said all in one big breath. I liked her a lot. She had a kind smile.

"Hello, Mrs. Hanako. Wow, what happened to your leg?" I asked, suddenly wondering if I was being impolite.

"Oh, it's broken, but the doctor said it will heal very quickly—it's not a bad break and it doesn't hurt too much," she answered. "But what about you three? Where have you been and why are your faces so dirty?" Her face was serious, but sad. "Well, anyway, who cares, as long as you are safe! We were so worried about you! Give me a hug."

Both Amanda and I rushed over and carefully gave her a hug, avoiding touching her leg.

"We had such an adventure, Mommy, you wouldn't believe it, and if you won't give me a 'time out,' I will tell you all about it!" said Maya.

"Oh, my dear one, I would never give you 'time out' for getting saved or saving yourself, no matter what you had to go through!" she said, as she hugged us all again, closing her eyes and smiling as tears rolled down her cheeks. "I am so glad to have you back in my arms!"

Then Maya looked at her mom's face and said, "Guess who's in this hospital, Mommy?"

"Well, I know your dad is here on the fourth floor, and he is going to be fine, don't worry!"

"Oh, yes, I want to go there right now and give him a hug!" said Maya.

"Well, you can just do that, Maya-chan, and he is so anxious to see you."

"Yeah, but do you know who else is here?" I asked.

"Who?" asked Maya's mother.

"My father!" I said, proudly.

"Well, you better go see him right away, because I am sure he is very worried about you too, and misses you very much."

"Maya made us promise to see you first, so here we are, but I think I need to go see my dad now, okay?" I said, as I brushed my hair away from my forehead.

"Of course, Elizabeth, and maybe you can look in on Maya's dad at the same time. They are on the same floor," said Yoko Hanako.

"Okay, come on, Amanda, let's go, and come on, Maya, you promised we wouldn't stay too long," I said, pulling Maya's hand.

Maya gave her mom a big kiss and her mom gave her a bigger kiss right back. Their eyes twinkled, as they looked at each other, so glad to touch each other again, and feel each other's breath, and hear each other's voices.

We all turned and went to the door, waving at Maya's mother. Brenda was waiting there for us, and she said she would take us to our dads.

Daddies

"Daddy, Daddy, Daddy," I said as I ran into his hospital room. He was sitting there with a bandage around his head. His arms were outstretched towards us.

I laid my head on his shoulder as I wrapped my arms tightly around him.

"Oh, Daddy, I missed you so much." I checked his face. He was smiling, so I continued. "I rowed our boat, and swam in the cold water with a dog, and remembered everything you ever taught me when we were at the lake," I said all in one breath, looking him straight in the eyes.

"Oh, my girls, my girls," said our dad. "I have been so worried about you. Thank God you are here and safe and sound," he said, wiping a tear from his eye. After he held us both at the same time very tightly, he held us both at arm's length, and looked at our faces to see our eyes and smiles, which, I could tell, he had missed very much.

"Were you scared without us?" he asked us.

"I was scared, Daddy, but I had my teddy bear and Elizabeth's, too," said Amanda, holding up the bears. "But I was really scared without you. Where were you?" she asked, with a slight angry look in her eyes.

"Amanda, we wanted so much to find you. We were in a huge mudslide at the Community Center and the whole side of the building caved in and many people were almost buried alive. The helicopter pilots got everyone out safely, but it was very scary for us, and hard for people to save us. But they did, and we were actually very lucky."

"We know. We saw the mess when we got to the Community Center. We saw our car, turned over. It was horrible, Daddy!" I said.

"Oh, dear," replied Dad. "I didn't know about the car. Well, when we were in the hospital we told the police about you and they tried to find you. Our cell phone got lost. We were so worried, wondering where you were. They couldn't find you at our house. They were searching for you in helicopters, but they couldn't find you. We were so frightened about what had happened to you! Another tear rolled down his cheek, as he pulled us close to his heart. "I am so, so happy to have you here in my arms, my wonderful children."

"I was scared, too, Daddy," I said. "I'm so glad you and Mommy are okay! I missed you both so much every minute and wanted you to tell me what to do. I thought you were looking for us. I didn't think you had been in an accident." There was a little silence and then I added, "But, you know what, Daddy, even though I missed you so much and I was scared, mostly it was kind of fun, after I forgot about being scared. We had fun in the boat, and climbing into people's windows, and swimming with a great dog. But I was scared a lot, Daddy," I said, hugging him.

I am sure my face revealed part of the story, as I momentarily drifted into the amazing recent adventures we had had in our red boat. I felt my eyebrows crease and my eyes widen as I thought about the scary moments when I had wondered where my parents were.

"Well, here we are now all together, with your mom remembering you and me, finally! She just phoned me. I knew she was in a coma, but now look what you children have accomplished! It was so amazing to hear her voice again and to know she remembered you children and me! It looks like she was not seriously hurt! She was very sleepy. She said it seemed like a second had passed, but also it seemed like a year to her. Did you know your mom lost her memory for a while?" he asked me.

"Yeah, she seemed a little dreamy, Daddy. But she got all excited when she saw us and then she remembered you, too! Just kidding!" I patted his shoulder.

"Oh, I am so glad!" he laughed. "Well, I think all she needed was to see her girls again. I am very, very, very happy you are all safe and sound!"

"Dad, when can we go home?" Amanda asked him, holding both bears under her free arm.

"Soon, Mandy," he said. "But we have to wait another few days until we can get out of the hospital and a couple of months after the waters go down so we can get the house repaired. I bet we'll have a big mess to clean up just like all the neighbors will, too."

"We know a neighbor called Mrs. Hendricks," Maya said. "We ate her food."

"And we know another neighbor who has golden puppies, and I want one," Amanda added.

"Puppies!" exclaimed Dad. "Well, we'll have to ask your mother about that."

"No, she said we had to ask you," Amanda said.

"Oh, well, in that case … I guess you can have a puppy, Amanda."

"Yes! Oh, goody! Oh, yes!" Amanda almost yelled.

Suddenly a big, sleepy voice from behind the curtains on the far side of the room, said, "Is that my little girl I hear?"

"Daddy, Daddy! Are you in there?" Maya asked.

"Your dad is right in here," he said as he wiggled the curtain.

Maya ran to the curtain and drew it back, and there was her dad, just trying to sit up, and with a head bandage on, just like my daddy. He looked like he was just waking up from a nap. Maya threw her arms around him.

"Oh, Daddy, I missed you so much! We had such an adventure. You won't believe it!" said Maya, inspecting his bandage and eyes.

"Yes, I will. I want to hear all about it," said Mr. Hanako, caressing Maya's unwashed face and dirty, windblown hair.

They hugged and kissed and looked into each other's eyes. Then they hugged another big hug. I saw Maya cry a little, and I saw her Daddy's mouth looking sad.

"Oh, Daddy," Maya started out. "Do you think I could have a ...." She looked at him, studying his face.

"... have a puppy?" he finished her sentence. "That's what woke me up—the idea of a puppy for my brave daughter. If it is all right with your mom, of course you can."

We three girls looked at each other with very big smiles, glad to be friends, and happy to have the little puppies coming into our lives.

THE FLOOD

Mrs. Hendricks

The waters did subside, and the people all came back to their muddy houses. There was mangled junk everywhere. There were soggy mattresses, pillows, dolls, carpets, and things starting to turn moldy and green. There were socks and shoes turned sideways and limp, and there were old boxes of detergent, wet and torn with bubbles all around them. There were all kinds of wet papers everywhere—newspapers and typing paper and limp-looking books.

I heard about some cats and sheep and more cows that drowned. It was hard for all the people to accept. Garbage men came by and got rid of them. The people started in cleaning everything up right away. It seemed to make them feel better just to be able to do something, and often for their neighbors first. Carpenters came from far and wide to help us replace the downstairs walls. Fortunately the upper story was not harmed, so, after it was all dry again, we could move upstairs and not live in a motel, but we still ate out every day!

There was a feeling of friendliness in the people that seemed unusual to me. People smiled at each other and were so glad to help each other out. I think they were glad everybody was still alive after the flood and the mudslide!

Trucks had come to take away the soaked and torn furniture and all the things that floated around from the houses and garages that were too wet to be any good any more. Maya told me that once they were told they could move back in Ginny purred for a whole day straight, she was so happy to be home.

We decided to go over to Mrs. Hendricks' house as soon as we could. Mom was now able to come with us, but Mrs. Hanako was still healing her leg, so she had to stay home.

We walked down the muddy, winding, tree-lined street and studied the treetops that we now knew so well. When we arrived at the house, we looked up on the side of the house where the high-water mark was still visible. We knocked on the door. Mom waited back at the road.

"Hello? Who's there?" asked Mrs. Hendricks, opening the door. Inside, carpenters were hammering and sawing.

"*We* are, Mrs. Hendricks. Hello. We're the ones who ate your food, and we want to thank you for putting it out! That food probably saved our lives! Well, at least it made our adventure a lot more yummy!" I said. I had been rehearsing this speech for days.

"Why, come on in and have some cookies," she said. "I am so very happy that someone got to eat that food, especially you young girls."

"Well, actually, we are going to see our puppies that we got from another house right now," said Maya, smiling like she had just secretly licked a little icing from a cake, and who really wanted to go see her puppy immediately.

"Well, you must take some cookies with you then—just a moment." Mrs. Hendricks walked into her kitchen and brought out a bag full of packaged cookies. The floodwater was all gone, but her yard was still muddy. We were standing on cardboard, which someone had laid down for people to walk on. There were people cleaning up all over her house. But she still had not run out of cookies!

"Thank you very, very much. It was really nice of you to put out food for somebody like you did," I said. We each took a chocolate chip cookie from the bag and took a bite.

"Well, I am so glad to know you girls, and so happy you got to eat the food. Next time you drop by, I will bake the cookies myself. Now, run along and see your puppies! Be sure to come by again," she added, as she stood by the door waving.

"Okay, goodbye, and thanks again," we said as we went to Mom who was still waiting by the curb. Everybody waved. We walked down the road munching our cookies and in another forty minutes we came to the house of the Golden Retrievers.

The Puppies

"**M**om, you have to come in with us this time," I said.

"Okay, let's go knock at the door," she said.

All three of us girls, with Mommy walking a little behind us, walked up to the front door of the house and we all knocked on the door at the same time. It was still muddy and dirty. A woman holding a baby came to the door. She must be the one they wrote the note to.

"Hello, are you the three young ladies who helped my dogs out?" she asked.

All of us had our hands behind our backs, and we all nodded firmly.

"I've seen you before, but never had a chance to talk to you. Well, come on in and see how the puppies are doing," she said. She led the way. We all followed her up the stairs and into the bedroom closet, their new, soft bed.

There were the puppies, all asleep, cuddled up against Goldie.

"I know which one is mine," Amanda said.

"No, you don't, they all look the same," Maya said, searching for the one she loved.

"Here's my puppy," Amanda said, bending down and petting the one near the mom's head. The mother dog looked up at Amanda, and stared right into Amanda's eyes. Amanda stared back. Then she slowly picked up her puppy as she stared into Goldie's eyes. Goldie's head moved forward and licked her puppy.

"It's okay," said Amanda gently. "I won't hurt her. Good dog. It's okay." Amanda brought the little, light golden puppy slowly up to her cheek and rocked it back and forth, her head tilted. "This one's mine," she told Mom. "Her name is Pumpkin."

Maya picked up a puppy, too. It's eyes opened and it yawned a very big, puppy yawn.

"This one's mine," she said, kissing the side of its forehead. The puppy licked her cheek, and she smiled and cradled it. "I am going to call it …" she paused. She looked underneath to check if it was a girl. "I am going to call her Susu."

I looked at the girls holding their puppies and secretly wished I could have my own puppy, but I knew we could only have one dog. So I smiled and held onto the one I loved, and tried to be brave and love Amanda's puppy.

"Well, Elizabeth, which one would you like?" said my mother.

"Mom, really? Could I have my own puppy?" I asked, holding my puppy to my cheek.

"You have earned it, Elizabeth, so go ahead and pick your own puppy," smiled my mom, putting her hand on my shoulder. She and Dad had been so flabbergasted to hear our story.

"This one's my favorite," I said, holding up the wiggly, very fluffy puppy that I was cuddling. "And I think his name is Lucky," I added, taking a quick peak under his tummy. "I think Daddy will like this one the best," I teased Amanda.

"Pumpkin and I can play together forever and love each other forever, just like I love you, Elizabeth," said Amanda, as she put her puppy next to my puppy. They licked each other's noses.

Normal Again

"Please pass the butter," I said, delighted to be sitting at our new breakfast table in our new kitchen. I was so tired of restaurants for the past two months!

We heard some squealing from the living room. Pumpkin and Lucky were tumbling along our new carpet and one must have hurt himself. I jumped up and ran to them. By the time I got there, they were standing before me, tongues out, almost smiling, and looking at me with those great big eyes!

"Good puppies!" I said, petting each one's head, and went back to finish my cereal. On my last bite, with the puppies now down by our heels hoping for crumbs, the doorbell rang.

Amanda jumped up this time and ran to the door and opened it wide. There stood Maya, with a broad smile, holding her own yellow puppy, and squeaking, "Hello! Here we are!" She stepped inside toward our puppies. Susu wiggled out of her arms and started leaping around her two siblings until it looked like a new kind of dance.

"Susu! Pumpkin! Lucky!" we called to the puppies to run into the living room. They jumped in and out of the new beds we had made out of blankets.

"Come and clear your plates!" Dad yelled. We skipped back into the kitchen, which seemed to glitter with new pots and pans hanging on the wall.

"Tonight we can play our new video," Mom said.

"What is it?" asked Maya.

"That's a secret," Mom said.

"It's not *The Wizard of Oz*," moaned Amanda. Mom shook her head.

"It's not *The Lion King*," said Maya. Again, Mom shook her head.

"You're staying home tonight, aren't you?" I asked.

"Of course!" Mom and Dad said at the same time.

I didn't particularly want to know what video it was. I decided to wait and let it be a surprise. I was just so happy and grateful to have our home back together, even the grandfather clock, and to have that safe feeling I used to have before the flood. And I was so happy to be back with Mom and Dad, Maya and Amanda and finally back home with our frisky, cuddly puppies: Susu, Pumpkin and Lucky!

THE END

Acknowledgements

As always, the first acknowledgement goes to my wonderful daughter, Elizabeth Stark, a great writer and teacher who has guided me every step of my journey with her wise feedback. Nanou Matteson, who was once a part of my writers' group and also one of my wonderful teachers, deserves a hearty thanks. My writers' group is, of course, my mainstay and many thanks go to those who used to be in it, and those who remain to this day: Marilynn Rowland, Sarita Berg, Dean Curtis, Ruth Hanham, Doris Fine, Elizabeth Greene, Joyce Scott, Carol Nyhoff, Karen Bird and others. Thanks go to the many friends who helped me feel okay with the drawings, especially my brother, Tom Gilb, who said I was the illustrator I was looking for.

I would like to thank my editor, Joe Miller, and my friends and advisers at BAIPA in Marin, especially Val Sherer, who helped with the cover and inside graphics and general good advice. Thanks go to Desiree DeOrto for help with the cover.

Special thanks to Ruth Schwartz for getting this to the final stages and making it real!

I would like to thank and acknowledge all the people who run The San Francisco Writers Conference, and, in particular, Michael Larsen, Elizabeth Pomada and Laurie McLean, for the many ways in which they have changed my life as I wrote and volunteered for many years since 2008.

Thanks to all of you who have read this book and written reviews, the author's gold, especially Leo and Charlie! And to Angie Powers for her amazing author photograph!

About the Author

Wendy started singing and writing folk songs in her teens. She has always written poetry and has had some poems published in the San Francisco Writers Conference Anthology and the Redwood Writers Anthology. She has been a teacher of young children for many years, has written, illustrated and published a few children's books, and also writes YA and adult novels. Wendy is interested in the Indie publishing world and is a member of the Bay Area Independent Publishers Association (BAIPA) and the Independent Book Publishers Association (IBPA). Her daughter, Elizabeth Stark, is a traditionally published writer, a well-respected online writing teacher and also teaches writing in person in the Bay Area. (BookWritingWorld.com).

Wendy Bartlett won second prize at the San Francisco Writers Conference for the manuscript for *Cellini's Revenge: The Mystery of the Silver Bowls*.

With the prize, part of which was a publishing package, she published first *Broad Reach,* a sailing adventure, and two years later, *Cellini's Revenge.* At the time of this writing, *Cellini's Revenge II* is in the process of being edited and *Cellini's Revenge III* is in the process of being written. An editor from BAIPA told Wendy that *Goodbye With a Kiss,* her most recent novel, might make a good film. Wendy is currently writing the screenplay for it.

kensingtonhillbooks.com

Made in the USA
Middletown, DE
04 January 2020